STILLMAN'S WAR

Ben Stillman 9

PETER BRANDVOLD

WOLFPACK PUBLISHING
— EST 2013 —

WOLFPACK
PUBLISHING
— EST 2013 —

Cover photography by Rick Evans Photography

Published in the United States by Wolfpack Publishing, Las Vegas

Wolfpack Publishing
6032 Wheat Penny Avenue
Las Vegas, NV 89122

wolfpackpublishing.com

Paperback ISBN 978-1-64119-630-7
eBook ISBN 978-1-64119-629-1

STILLMAN'S
WAR

Chapter One

BEN STILLMAN, SHERIFF of Hill County in the vast northern Montana Territory, slipped his ivory-gripped Colt revolver from its soft leather California holster angled for the cross-draw on his left hip and checked the loads. He plucked a .44-caliber bullet from his shell belt and slid it through the open loading gate, filling the one empty chamber that had been resting beneath the hammer.

Now all six chambers showed brass.

Stillman flicked the loading gate closed with his gloved right thumb and spun the cylinder.

"How you wanna play it, Ben?" asked his deputy, Leon McMannigle, who sat his steeldust gelding to Stillman's right.

Their breaths plumed in the chill night air.

October had come to the Two-Bear Mountains, a northern Montana "island" range sitting in isolation from the high, massives ridges of the Rocky Mountain spine jutting farther west. Dead leaves occasionally fell from the cotton-woods, aspens and box elders lining Loco Jack Creek, which ran through the trees and brush to the left of the lawmen. The creek gurgled and tittered over rocks edged with thin shards of starlight-reflecting ice. The falling leaves made a soft ratcheting sound as they landed.

The cold air was stitched with the smell of burning cottonwood.

"Oh, I don't know," Stillman said lazily. "How 'bout like we always do? I take the front and you take the back?"

"You know, Ben, sometimes I'd like to try the front door for a change."

"Front door's usually hotter." Stillman swung down from his saddle and slid his Henry repeater from its scabbard. "But, hell, if you feel slighted, you can go in the front door . . . and I'll take the back."

He arched a salt-and-pepper brow at his friend and deputy.

Leon stared off through the trees, in the direction from which the wood smoke was emanating. "Ah, hell," he said finally, running a black-gloved hand down his cheek of the same color. "I reckon I'm just romanticizin' a front door entrance. And since I'm so used to the back door, might as well not fix what works."

He reached back and down to slide his Winchester carbine from his own saddle boot jutting over left saddlebag pouch. "What time you want to do-si-do in the kitchen?"

Stillman slipped his Ingersoll watch from his pocket and flipped the lid. "It's about ten forty-five. How about eleven-fifteen? Give us plenty of time to get situated."

Leon reached inside his blue-and-black plaid wool mackinaw and fished his old, battered railroad turnip from the breast pocket of his hickory shirt. He flipped the lid. "Ten forty-five it is." He adjusted his own watch and dropped the turnip back into his pocket.

Stillman quietly pumped a cartridge into his Henry's action. "You sure you don't want the front door? I don't want you to feel insulted or anything. Back door sounds fine as frog hair to me."

Leon showed the whites of his eyes in the darkness. "Nah, nah. Now that I think on it, I've always been a back door sorta fella, anyways. Just shy, I reckon. Yep, I'm more comfortable enterin' the back door than the front. Besides, you're the sheriff and I'm your deputy, and shame on me for questioning your methods, Ben!"

Leon jerked his black, broad-brimmed hat down low over his eyes, reined his steeldust around, and trotted the horse off in the darkness, following the slow curve of the creek.

Stillman gave a wry snort as he watched the former buffalo soldier disappear in the darkness, the creek glittering like a black snakeskin in its sheath of brush and trees. When McMannigle's soft hoof thuds had dwindled to silence, Stillman led his fine, broad-barreled bay, Sweets, over to a dead tree and tossed the reins over a spidery limb.

"Stay, boy," he said, patting the horse's long, sleek neck. "You stay and don't let anyone sneak up on us from behind, all right? Okay, then . . ."

Sweets gave a low whicker and sniffed Stillman's high-crowned tan Stetson. The stallion obviously knew what was happening. He'd been through it all before many times--him waiting while his rider ran down border toughs and owlhoots. Usually after a considerable amount of shooting. Stillman wondered if the horse ever anticipated a time when, after the shooting, Stillman did not return and Sweets was left on his own.

Stillman himself did. There had been a time when he did not think about such things, like back when he was a young, hot-headed, hard-pounding Deputy U.S. Marshal running down federal criminals throughout the territory from the Milk River in the north to the Powder in the south, from the towering peaks of the Rockies in the west to the sandy bluffs and wide, muddy streams in the east.

Now, though, pushing fifty and married and with a bun in his wife's, Faith's, oven, he probably thought about it too much. That was the problem with getting old. You started to think about what you had to lose. At least you did if you'd acquired such things as a loving wife and the promise of a family.

Things you sure as hell didn't want to lose.

A fear of mortality was not always a lawman's friend. It made you overly cautious and thoughtful at time when it was best for your instincts to guide you. Fear, and the thinking that resulted from it, could get you killed.

Stillman shoved all that mind rot aside. At least as far to one side as possible given his unbridled delight at the thought that he'd soon have either a son or a daughter and his fear of missing out on that experience. That he and Faith, his young and beautiful French wife born and raised in the Powder River country, would have a boy to raise on their humble little chicken ranch on the bluffs north of Clantick.

The big, broad-shouldered sheriff clad in a buckskin mackinaw and a knit green scarf wrapped around his neck inside his coat, moved off into the brush and stopped just inside the dark columns of the trees at the edge of the creek. He brushed his hand across his nose and bushy, salt-and-pepper mustache and stared beyond the creek, listening hard. His breath plumed in gray puffs around his head.

The old Turner cabin was about fifty yards beyond the rippling, glinting water. That's where he and McMannigle had decided the four or five rustlers who'd been preying on the northern Two-Bears for the past three months had been holing up when they weren't driving small herds of stolen beeves up to Canada. Stillman and Leon had come upon the place when the rustlers hadn't been there, though there'd been plenty of cow tracks around the place, and they'd found fresh food leavings and split firewood inside the ramshackle cabin. They'd also found two running irons and a carbine.

Running irons were what long-loopers used to touch up the brands on the cattle they stole.

Now, tonight, it was time to put the rustlers out of commission.

Stillman found a rocky ford just upstream and crossed the creek, barely getting his boots wet.

He moved quietly through the woods, weaving around black tree columns and avoiding thick clumps of brush. His nose was filled with the cool, loamy tang of the forest. Occasionally, he scented the smoke from the cabin. His boots crackled softly on the soft forest floor. Often, especially at times like these, he wished he could move as quietly as an Indian and wondered how in hell they did that.

He'd just spied the flickering lights of the cabin windows when a warbling, windy sound rose before him, growing quickly louder. Instinctively, he ducked sharply, dropped to one knee, and felt the brush of displaced air against the crown of his hat a moment before something thudded into the broad elm tree he'd just stepped around. He glanced over his shoulder and up to see the handle of the axe embedded in the tree still quivering.

He whipped his head forward. Boots crunched and thudded. A shadow darted between him and the windows of the shake-shingled cabin, crouching in the darkness fifty feet away in a small clearing. Twenty feet ahead of Stillman was a chopping block and a small pile of freshly split stove wood.

The man sprinting toward the cabin shouted, "Law trouble, boys! Law trouble! Grab your guns and start *shootin'!*"

The shrill voice echoed around the clearing, pitched with a mixture of anxiousness and cocky amusement. The shadow stopped suddenly between Stillman and a window. The man reached for a rifle that had been leaning against the cabin's front porch, and, quickly pumping a cartridge into the chamber, wheeled toward Stillman.

The sheriff shouted, *"Law!* Throw the gun down!"

The announcement and admonition were perfunctory. Stillman knew the rustler wasn't going to heed the warning. That's why the lawman had already pressed his Henry's brass butt plate to his shoulder and was squeezing the trigger before "down!" had even left his lips.

The Henry thundered loudly, smoke and flames lapping toward the cabin. The rustler gave a choked, *"Ohh!"* and stumbled back toward the porch, firing his own rifle into the air. He fell backward and smacked his head with a resolute thud against the front of the porch and rolled sideways onto his belly, giving strangled wails.

Shouts and the loud thumps of stomping boots rose from the cabin. Shadows jostled behind lamplit windows.

Stillman took about one second to reconsider his strategy and then, ejecting the spent, smoking shell casing from his Henry's breech and levering a live one into the action, bounded off his heels and started running toward the cabin.

"Leon, I'm goin' in now!" he shouted, lifting his knees high to avoid tripping over some unseen obstacle in the darkness, holding the Henry high across his chest.

The door burst open and a shadow edged in lamplight lurched out onto the porch. There was the raking, metallic rasp of a rifle being cocked, and then lamplight winked off the barrel as the man on the porch raised his rifle to his shoulder.

Stillman stopped, dropped to a knee, shouted "Hold it!" again perfunctorily, and squeezed the Henry's trigger even as he yelled it. The man on the porch grunted. His own rifle barked and flashed, sending a round screeching two feet to Stillman's right and loudly hammering a tree behind him, flinging bark in all directions.

The rustler gave a croaking sound as he bounced off the doorframe, and, dropping his rifle, twisted around and fell just inside the cabin's open door. Even before he hit, Stillman was off running, wincing a little at a stitch in his right knee—he wasn't as young as he used to be and he'd never been light on his feet—and mounted the porch in one leaping stride.

There was much shouting and screaming and boot pounding inside the cabin. As the big sheriff crossed the porch, there was the screech of shattering glass as someone broke out a window to his left.

As two rifles began barking inside the cabin, Stillman hurled himself through the open door, leaping the stocky dead man still quivering over the doorjamb. Stillman hit the puncheon floor on his right shoulder, raising the cocked Henry from his left hip.

A man was just then turning from the front window. Another was turning from a window beyond him, on the cabin's far side, where that man had been crouching over a rickety rocking chair.

The first man cursed and fired his Winchester carbine, but the bullet merely blew slivers off the edge of the table strewn with bottles, plates, glasses, and food leavings and that offered Stillman partial cover. Stillman fired from his right hip but because his momentum was still sliding him across the floor toward the dark mouth of a narrow stairs rising to the second story, his bullet flew wide of its mark.

"You son of a buck!" the tall, gangly man with a colorless goat beard bellowed as he snapped off another shot.

The bullet hammered into the wall as Stillman gained a heel and threw himself behind the sheet iron stove on top of which a cast-iron pot bubbled bean juice up around its rattling lid. He raised his Henry over the top of the stove, fired, and evoked a resounding yelp from the man on the other side of the table.

Seeing the other man, harder to Stillman's right now, aim his own rifle at him, Stillman jerked his head back behind the stove's broad, tin chimney. The second shooter's bullet blew the pot of beans off the stove and onto the floor over the sheriff's left shoulder. The man's second bullet clanked loudly off the front of the iron stove. The man on the other side of the table yelped again as the ricochet plunked into his belly with a dull thump.

"Oh!" he screamed, lowering his arms and dropping his chin to look at the blood oozing out of the hole in his checked wool shirt, between the flaps of his cracked, black leather vest. His dark eyes were wide and bright with horror.

"Oh, now! Ohhh! *Ohhhhh!*"

His caterwauling distracted the second shooter—a tall man with very long, dark-brown hair hanging over a beaded elkhide tunic. He wore a tall, bullet-crowned black hat. Stillman raised his Henry and sent the man hurling backward through the window at that end of the cabin. He sort of folded up like a jackknife and took his leave of the hovel in a screech of breaking glass.

He landed with a deep thud outside the cabin, and Stillman heard him expel a muffled grunt even beneath what the lawman now realized were a girl's hysterical screams emanating from the cabin's second story.

Chapter Two

STILLMAN REMOVED HIS hat and edged a look around the door to the stairwell.

He peered up the steep, short wooden stairs to see a pale, naked, bearded man aiming two pistols at him from the top of the steps. The armed man angled both revolvers down over the stairs, both hammers cocked.

Stillman jerked his head back as both pistols barked and tore two, large divots of wood from the casing, one sliver pricking Stillman's right cheek. The girl continued screaming at the tops of her lungs behind the naked, bearded shooter.

"Come on out, lawman," the naked gunman shouted. "Or I'll kill this little doxie up here!"

Doxie?

Stillman hadn't realized they had a girl until he'd heard the screams.

He set his Henry aside and yelled, "Hold on, hold on, for chrissakes! Who's the girl?"

He slipped his Colt from its holster, clicked the hammer back.

"Nothin' more'n a side of purty beef if you don't throw your guns down and get out here where I can see you!"

The girl screamed louder.

"All right, all right!" Stillman snaked his pistol around the side of the door casing, keeping the barrel nudged up taut against the wood. He glanced around the casing to get his bearings and then pulled his head back and triggered his Colt once, twice, three times, shouting, "Here you go, you son of a buck!"

The shooter triggered both his own pistols once more after Stillman's second shot, the two bullets tearing into the floor at the bottom of the stairs. Stillman heard him groan.

As the sheriff pulled his revolver back away from the door casing, there were a full two seconds of silence before he heard the thunder of a body rolling violently down the stairs. He glanced to his left to see the naked shooter come tumbling out of the doorway and turning a forward somersault into the kitchen, where he lay flat on his back, spread-eagle, eyes open.

His mouth opened and closed inside his beard, like a fish's. Blood trickled out one corner of it to stain the dark red hair on his chin. Blood also oozed from the three holes in his pale, bony torso.

He gave a jerk, sighed, and lay still.

Stillman slid his head halfway around the casing again, cocking the Colt and aiming it up the stairs—at nothing but a low stretch of scarred, wooden ceiling across which dull, umber lamplight wavered from somewhere ahead and to the right. He could hear someone stumbling around up there, breathing hard.

The girl had stopped screaming and was now only whimpering loudly in the close quarters that smelled of sour sweat, a kerosene lamp, and a charcoal brazier.

"Shut up, you crazy devil!" a man's voice barked.

The girl mewled.

Stillman climbed the stairs slowly, stretched his gaze over the top in time to see a half-dressed man climb out a window ahead and on his right, near a bed covered in pelts and atop which a pale, sandy-haired girl sat with her back against a wall, naked, her head resting in her arms atop her upraised knees.

"Stop, or I'll blow you to hell!" Stillman shouted.

The half-dressed man swung around toward Stillman, a pistol in his hand. His free arm was loaded down with clothes and a pair of saddlebags. He was wearing a hat, which shaded the top half of his face. His pistol flashed and barked.

Stillman pulled his head down below the top of the stairs as the slug chewed into the floor two feet ahead of him. When he looked up the stairs again, the man was gone. Stillman heard a crunching thud, felt the slight reverberation beneath his boots on the stairs. Apparently, the man had leaped onto a lower outside roof.

Stillman bolted up the stairs. Halfway to the window, he heard Leon shout, "Stop right there or you're a dead man, amigo!"

There were two quick reports, one practically on top of the other one. There was a muffled grunt. Stillman crouched to peer through the window, saw a shadow dash off into the woods behind the cabin.

"Leon!"

"Ben, you all right?" the deputy called up from somewhere unseen in the dark yard below.

"Unhurt. How 'bout yourself?"

"Fine as frog hair. I think I pinked that son of a buck. All clear in there?"

"Yeah."

Stillman pulled his head out of the window and turned to the girl who was staring at him with a combination of terror and relief over the tops of her upraised knees. She was naked and pale, and she was clamping one arm across her chest. A tuft of hair and a bit of pink shone between her legs, down low against the pelt she was sitting on.

Stillman looked quickly away from it, shame briefly warming his ears.

Frowning, he said, "What's your name, Miss?"

"Orlean Hollister," she said in a little girl's pain- and horror-pinched voice, tears dribbling down her pretty, pale cheeks. "Those men . . . they . . . they kidnapped me from my father's ranch!"

Stillman moved over to her, lowering his smoking Colt. "Watt Hollister's daughter?" Hollister was one of the largest, most respected ranchers in Hill County, his vast holdings spilling down the Two Bear Mountains' western flanks toward the breaks of the Missouri River. His gaze encompassed nearly ten thousand acres, and, depending on the time of year, he had anywhere between twenty and thirty riders on his payroll.

The girl nodded, lowered her face again to her knees, and sobbed. "Oh, god—what they did to me! Over and over! I'm so *ashamed*!"

Stillman patted the girl's shoulder. The warm room reeked of coal, man-sweat, musty pelts, whiskey, and sex—if you could call it that. "It'll be all right. We'll get you back home."

Boots thudded below and a voice called up the stairs, "Ben?"

"I'll be right down." Stillman squeezed one

of the girl's hands. "It'll be all right. Why don't you go ahead and get dressed and we'll get you on the trail back to Clantick? Should be there by morning."

The girl lifted her tear-streaked face and pinched her pain-racked, light-brown eyes. She had about five freckles on the nubs of her pale, plump cheeks and a thumb-shaped birthmark on her neck. She sniffed and said beseechingly, "I couldn't help what they done . . . made me do." She clamped Stillman's hand desperately in her own. "They said they'd kill me and send me back in pieces to the ranch. I didn't want . . . I couldn't let my mother and father go through that!"

"It's all right," Stillman repeated, placing a comforting hand on the back of the girl's head. "No one will blame you for this. Your folks will understand."

Staring at him, the girl drew her lips into her mouth and tried a smile.

"Go ahead and get dressed," Stillman said, giving her back a couple of soft, reassuring pats.

As Stillman turned away from the bed, he heard the stairs creak and a spur ching.

"Everything all right up here?" Leon said.

The deputy's black hat and dark face rose up into Stillman's view from the dark stairwell.

Stillman stopped in front of the stairs, and

sighed. "Well, sort of." He glanced over his shoulder.

With his boots planted halfway up the stairs, Leon glanced around the cluttered, smelly, dimly lit half-story room, frowning. "The backdoor was blocked by firewood, Ben," he said absently.

Stillman gave an ironic chuff. "Yeah, I considered that possibility . . . when I was halfway to the cabin."

Leon's eyes settled on the girl, and then he looked at Stillman, wrinkling the skin above the bridge of his nose. "Who . . .?"

"Watt Hollister's daughter."

Stillman took one step down the stairs. Leon had started to turn and start down himself when, glancing around once more, his wide, molasses-dark eyes widened until they were nearly all whites, and he shouted, "Ben, *down!*"

Stillman threw himself forward and sideways. Behind him, a gun crashed loudly. As Stillman hit the floor to the right of the stairwell, he saw Leon snap up his Schofield .44, extending it straight out from his shoulder. The Schofield flashed and roared as the gun behind Stillman barked once more.

At the same time, the girl screamed.

Lying prone, Stillman turned his head, whipping his longish, salt-and-pepper hair from his

eyes to see the girl fly back onto the bed, dropping a small, smoking pistol onto the floor with
a dull thud. She lay back on the bed, still naked.
Her pale, slender legs dangled toward the floor,
twitching.

Stillman stared, his lower jaw hanging in
shock. "I'll be . . . damned . . .!"

Leon stared wide-eyed over the smoking barrel of his still-extended Schofield. Very slowly,
he started to lower the gun. In a low, bewildered
rasp, he muttered, "She was . . . she was . . ."

He let his voice trail off.

Silence filled the half-story space cluttered
with old, moldering tack and mining supplies
left-over from the place's previous owner and
the occasional outlaw gangs who holed up in the
place from time to time, usually on their way
from some hold-up farther south and on their
way to Canada.

Stillman slowly gained his feet. Leaving Leon
standing statue-still in the stairwell, he walked
over to where the girl lay slumped on the bed.
She sat on her butt, her torso twisted onto one
shoulder, feet dangling about six inches above the
floor. Her feet were small and pale and slender.
She wasn't a very big girl. Stillman guessed she
didn't weight quite a hundred pounds. He'd heard
that Hollister had a daughter, but he'd never met

the girl. He'd met Hollister's three sons but never the girl. Hollister and his wife, Virginia, both native Texans, were known to keep the girl close to home. Virginia, nearly twenty years Watt's junior but as persnickety as a woman twice her age, was known to be devout.

Stillman placed his left hand on the girl's right shoulder and gently rolled her onto her back. Blood trickled through the shallow valley between them from the neat, round dimple in the middle of her chest, just above her breastbone.

The girl's eyes were wide open and staring, the flickering, umber lamplight wavering over them like light on a frozen pond. Her chest lay still. She was dead.

Watt Hollister's daughter was dead.

Floorboards creaked behind Stillman. Mc-Mannigle's spurs rattled faintly. "She was, she was . . ."

"I know," Stillman said, seeing the deputy's shadow elongate across the bed to the sheriff's left. "She was going to back-shoot me."

Stillman gave an inward shudder. He'd been backshot before by mistake by a drunk parlor girl. He cringed at the thought of it happening again. That bullet, still in his back, had closed the book on his career as a deputy United States marshal.

"Why?" Leon asked in dull exasperation as he stood beside Stillman.

Staring down at the girl, his ears ringing from confusion and all the gunfire in the tight confines, Stillman said, "She would have shot us both, if she'd had her way."

"But, why?"

"Maybe she wasn't as unhappy as she let on. About bein' a hostage."

"You think she went willingly with them rustlers?"

"I don't know. Maybe her father can help fill in the gaps. We'll get her back to the Triple H Connected, hear what he has to say."

"Holy crap in the nun's privy--I know what he's gonna have to say about me killin' his daughter!"

"Like I said, she would have killed us both—you after me. Why is what we have to find out." Stillman started to reach for the girl.

McMannigle nudged him, said, "Let me, Ben. I shot her."

Leon wrapped the girl in a large deerskin blanket, tucking both ends so that none of her pale, fragile-looking body was exposed, not even her hair. When he had picked the bundle up in his arms, he followed Stillman down the steps to the first floor where the three dead men lay.

McMannigle took the girl out onto the porch

while Stillman looked around. Blood was liber-ally splattered over the kitchen area of the cabin. A pair of saddlebags hung from a chair back near where the man who'd fired out the window lay slumped on his side against the front wall.

Stillman opened the flap of one of the bags, reached in, and pulled out several packets of greenbacks and silver certificates. He opened the flap on the other bag, and pulled out several more pouches.

"What you got there?" McMannigle asked as he stepped back into the cabin.

"The reason the Hollister girl wanted to fill us full o' lead," the sheriff said.

Chapter Three

Stillman drew a puff from his cigarette and blew the smoke up toward the rusty Rochester lamp hanging over the table by an equally rusty wire. The smoke hit the lamp and fanned out in a large, luminous cloud.

Stillman and McMannigle had dragged the dead rustlers off into the corral flanking the cabin, excepting the dead Hollister girl, who lay on a pallet in the rundown parlor. The lawmen didn't want wildcats or coyotes getting to her during the night. They didn't want to take a mangled corpse back to the Hollister ranch. They'd decided to catch forty winks here in the cabin and get a fresh start back to Clantick in the morning.

The sheriff was counting the money he'd found in the saddlebags. He tossed the last of the bills onto a stack on the table before him. "Eleven thousand four hundred and twenty . . . thirty . . .

forty . . . fifty . . . six and one more dollar makes eleven thousand four hundred and fifty-seven dollars. They really raked in the money, sellin' stolen stock up in Canada. I'm gonna have to ride up there one of these days and have a talk with the Mounties in Moose Jaw. See if they know who's buyin' long-looped Montana beef."

"Sizable chunk of change," Leon said, splashing more whiskey into the tin cup before him, a half-smoked cheroot smoldering in his gloved hand. "But mere chump change to the Hollisters."

The deputy splashed more whiskey into Stillman's cup and set the half-empty bottle down on the table. Stillman took another drag from his quirley and ran a hand through his thick, wavy hair, blowing smoke up at the lamp again. He took a sip of the whiskey, the comforting burn of which helped stave off the cold pushing through the broken window and shuttling a draft around the cabin despite the stove the lawmen had stoked.

"Yeah, it's odd for a rich girl to take up with raggedy-heeled owlhoots," Stillman said. "But I've seen crazier things in the half a lifetime I've lived so far."

McMannigle looked at the long, deerskin bundle lying on the floor near the small stone hearth in the parlor side of the cabin. They hadn't built a fire in the fireplace because, judging by the leaves and cobwebs in it, the chimney was likely blocked by birds' nests or leaf snags.

The Stanley place hadn't been a permanent home in several years, since Indians had driven the Stanleys out of this valley before Stillman had come out of retirement to become Hill County Sheriff. The land had since been bought by a neighboring rancher, but no one had moved back onto the headquarters—except itinerant bands of owlhoots, that was. Despite Stillman's best efforts, such curly wolves were still fairly common in this vast, remote northern part of a still wild and wooly territory.

"You suppose she took up with 'em because she was in love with one of 'em?" Leon asked as he stared forlornly at the bundle.

"There were two upstairs with her."

McMannigle turned to Leon, glowering. "Two?"

"Two."

"That delicate little white girl was taking two men at the same time?"

"Maybe she wasn't as delicate as she looks."

"Well, I'll be." Leon looked at the girl again and shook his head. "I wonder what old Watt Hollister would say about that."

"I'd heard old Hollister and his wife were right

protective of the girl. Sometimes that'll turn a girl . . . or a boy . . . as wild as a young coyote with the springtime itch. I'm bettin' that's what happened here. I don't know. We'll talk to the old man, get his side of it, try to get to the bottom of it."

"Could be these men rode for Hollister," Leon said.

"Could be."

"Maybe that's how they come to know little Miss."

"Could be."

McMannigle stared at the girl for a time and then slid his gaze back to Stillman. "You know her name, Ben?"

"She said it was Orlean. Orlean Hollister."

"Orlean"

"That's what she told me. I heard Virginia Hollister's family was originally from New Orleans."

Leon drew a deep, ragged breath and shook his head again. "Sure wish I hadn't had to shoot her."

"Well, you did have to." Stillman stretched his back with a wince, splashed more whiskey into his deputy's tin cup, and used the bottleneck to nudge the cup toward him encouragingly. "If you hadn't, you'd have my wife to contend with, and when she gets that French blood of hers up, you'd rather tangle with two hydrophobic wild cats in a Dougherty wagon."

McMannigle lowered his head and chuckled.

"Besides, she'd likely have drilled your ass, too. So call it self-preservation as opposed to suicide."

The deputy sighed, lowered his head again, and ran a hand over his close-cropped, wooly, black pate. "I just got a big problem with shootin' women, Ben. Especially young women. Especially young white women. You'd understand if you was black."

"You think I like shooting young white women?" Stillman grinned and mashed his quirley out on the table. "Drink up and let's get some sleep. Sun'll be up in a couple hours."

~~~

Stillman and McMannigle were up at first light.

They brewed a pot of coffee on the cabin's sheet-iron stove and breakfasted on the hot, black coffee, elk jerky they'd packed, and a can of tomatoes they found on a shelf in the cabin. Afterwards, they both smoked a cigarette out on the front porch, watching the sky turn green over the low, forested western ridges.

As they did, Stillman laid out his plan for the morning.

"You go ahead and start back to town with the girl and what's left of those owlhoots in the stable," he told Leon. "We'll throw them over their horses' backs and give Auld a few bucks to bury them if no one claims them, which I doubt anyone will."

"You're goin' after the man I wounded?"

Stillman nodded. "How bad did you wound him?"

"Couldn't tell but I heard him give a yelp. I got him, all right. Might be layin' up there, waitin' for us to pull out see if he can't get a hoss." McMannigle blew cigarette smoke out into the still-dark yard in which birds were chirping almost maniacally. It seemed to be increasing as the light intensified in the arching sky. "Might be dead, far as that goes."

"I'll check it out. Either way, I'll find him. And we won't be leavin' him any horses. All the horses will go with you. When I find him, I'll catch up with you."

"What about the girl?"

"We'll have Auld put her in a box, and I'll haul her out to the Triple H Connected, turn her over to her folks."

"I oughta do that. Explain it to her old man. I shot her."

"I'm the sheriff," Stillman said, giving his deputy a commanding look from beneath the brim of his broad tan Stetson, blowing cigarette smoke out his nostrils. "It's my job. You shot her in the line of duty, in self-defense, and that's enough of that conversation."

"Well, I oughta ride with you, anyway, Ben."

"We're the only two lawmen in this whole, damn county, Leon. And we have tracklayers from the railroad in town. You know what kind of a ruckus they can raise. It don't make sense for both of us to haul one dead girl way out to the backside of the Bear Paws. That's a two-day wagon ride, round trip."

Stillman shook his head and flicked his quirley into the yard. "No, I can't justify us both leavin' the office unattended after we already both been gone for two days. I'm goin' alone and, like I said, that's the end of that conversation."

He tossed the dregs of his coffee into the yard, adjusted his hat, set his cup on the porch rail, and moved down the porch steps to head for the corral and stable.

When the lawmen had gotten the dead men's horses saddled and the bodies tied over the saddles of their fidgety mounts, who didn't care for the smell of blood, they led the pack string, tied tail to tail, back to the cabin. They tied the dead Hollister girl over a blue roan, and Leon mounted his steeldust gelding with the roan's bridle reins in his hand.

"I'm hoping to catch up to you before you get to

Clantick," Stillman said.

"All right, then."

"Leon?"

McMannigle was still getting seated. "Yeah?"

Stillman glanced at the deerskin shrouding the dead Hollister girl. "Nothin'."

There was nothing he could say to ease his deputy's pain. Stillman would have felt the same way over shooting a girl, even one he'd been fully justified in shooting. Well, not the same way, exactly. Leon had the added complication of his having killed a white girl. Stillman knew he could never fully understand that part of it. He'd hold his tongue.

"You be careful, Ben. You know--a wounded wildcat, and all that." Leon pinched his hat brim.

The deputy turned forward in his saddle and touched spurs to his steeldust's flanks. The horse started off down a brushy two-track trail that curled west through the aspen and box elder woods and toward a bend in the quietly chuckling creek that skirted the ranch yard. The six horses with their grisly cargoes lurched forward and eased into walks before, leaving the yard as they passed a squat log shed with many holes in its roof, McMannigle spurred his own mount into a spanking trot, and the pack horses, tied tail to tail, begrudgingly followed suit.

Stillman watched the horses drift off along

the trail through the woods then went back to the stable to saddle Sweets. He left the bay tied outside the dilapidated, peeled pole corral while he looked around. He found some light blood splatters just behind a low-slung rear addition to the cabin. The addition was abutted by a long, high stack of freshly split firewood, as though the rustlers had planned to lay up here for a while.

Some of the logs were strewn about the base of the stack. The man who'd leaped out the window had apparently jumped onto the stack and then to the ground, where he'd encountered Leon and had taken a bullet from the deputy's Schofield. The ground was fairly hard-packed and littered with bits of old hay, oats, and straw, but Stillman managed to pick up the man's boot tracks and follow them to where he'd run around the west side of the corral and into the woods north of the ranch yard.

Stillman lost the boot prints in the trees but kept moving north until he found another streak of blood on a deadfall aspen. He kept walking north until the woods gave way to open ground—a brief stretch of blond prairie grass that rose gently toward the creek and its slim sheathing of autumn crimson chokecherries and sumacs and yellow river willows. The creek was shallow, so Stillman crossed it easily. After he'd gained the other side and had continued walking forty yards from the stream, looking for more tracks and more blood, he began feeling the burn of frustration.

He'd seen nothing since he'd left the creek.

He climbed to the top of the rise and looked down into a shallow valley with what appeared an arroyo running down the middle of it, parallel with the ridge Stillman was on. The ridges on either side of it were stippled with piñon pines, with a large, old, lightning-topped cottonwood standing farther down near the rocky streambed. A raptor of some kind—it looked like a golden eagle—sat hunched in its deep feathers on one of the charred limbs. The arroyo jogged down to Stillman's right for a hundred yards and then meandered away from him, toward the southeast and a swell of low, brown hills.

The arroyo would be a good, sheltered place for a wounded rustler to hole up in. Possibly die in. That eagle might be waiting to dine.

Stillman spat to one side, doffed his hat, and ran his hand through his hair that was sweaty now, as the day was heating up as the sun inched farther above the horizon. He had to recon the arroyo. He didn't want to, because he wanted to get back to Clantick and deal with the dead Hollister girl. Something told him that Leon might go against orders and take the girl back to the Triple H Connected on his own.

McMannigle was a loyal, invaluable deputy, and while he rarely went against Stillman's orders—in fact, the sheriff couldn't recollect when he ever had—Leon was pretty torn up about the girl. He felt the need to take responsibility for it, to explain the matter to her folks. Maybe, in a roundabout way, he was seeking forgiveness. An admirable attitude, of course, but also one that might get him killed.

Stillman just now realized that part of his reluctance about having his deputy ride out to the Hollister place was due to his fear of how Leon might be received.

A black man hauling the body of the white girl he'd killed back to her own people. Especially Southern people . . .

Still, the sheriff felt a strong obligation to investigate the arroyo. He didn't want to leave one of the rustlers at large and risk him getting away and possibly forming another bunch or seeking revenge for his dead accomplices. That would be like leaving a keg of dynamite out here with the fuse attached.

Stillman cursed, spat again, and tramped back down the rise and across the creek. He retrieved his bay stallion from the ranch yard, and, mounted, rode up and down the arroyo and along both of its brushy banks several times, looking for the wounded rustler. He rode for nearly ninety minutes, as far as a mile out along the streambed's southeast jog, and found nothing more interesting than a moldering, wheelless wagon rotting amongst the brush and rocks, and the bleached bones of several cows and one horse.

No blood. No footprints. No body.

Nothing.

Confounded, he rode straight south and investigated a coulee and another, shorter canyon. He found one sock, but it was so badly sun-faded and torn that, while it might have belonged to his quarry, he doubted it. It wasn't enough evidence to keep him out here any longer.

Cursing under his breath, Stillman turned Sweets toward home.

A vague apprehension had been eating at him for the past two hours. Suddenly, he was more worried about McMannigle than he was about finding the wounded rustler.

He hoped like hell that saving Stillman's life wouldn't get Leon killed.

Chapter Four

Several hours later, well past midday, Stillman pushed Sweets on into Clantick.

The little town, which was the seat of Hill County, sat amidst chalky, sage- and yucca-spiked buttes lining the Milk River, which meandered only a quarter mile north. It was near the river that Stillman's own, small chicken ranch perched on the shoulder of a flat-topped butte overlooking the dusty settlement that around twenty-five years ago had started out as a hide hunter's camp but had gradually been transformed into a ranch supply hub—one that would soon be connected by Northern Pacific rails not only to Chicago and points east, but to the West Coast as well.

Still, it remained a humble little village and home to only around a thousand or so souls—most of them good, hard-working souls though there were a few sour apples in every barrel. The mostly log but some adobe business buildings pushed up around Stillman now as he slowed his hard-ridden but stalwart bay to a walk, signs announcing the various businesses reaching into the street upon skinned pine poles.

Fallen cottonwood leaves skidded across the street, as did the occasional tumbleweed or newspaper torn from a trash heap.

There was a lot of horse and wagon traffic, and Stillman returned the greetings of several men he knew standing around outside of the harness shop, feed supply shop, Verne Gandy's Mercantile, and the town's several saloons. No less than a dozen saddle horses were tied to hitchracks fronting the two main watering holes, the Milk River Saloon and the Drovers. The din of loud conversation, laughter, and the patter of piano music swelled out over the saloons' louvred doors. There were the clinks of coins and the clatter of roulette wheels, which meant that the money the cow punchers had made from the various fall roundups was burning holes in the boys' pockets and was just now switching hands mighty quickly.

A girl's scream sounded from a Milk River Saloon second floor window, causing Stillman to jerk back on his horse's reins.

"Damn you, Pike," shouted the girl. "I told you

no free feels! You wanna squeeze my titties, you pay downstairs *first,* or get the hell out!"

A man's drunken voice gave a simpering retort, and Stillman booted Sweets on down the street. He'd recognized the voice of an aging parlor girl named Starr Brightly—she claimed it was her actual name—and the sheriff was confident that Miss Starr was capable of taking care of herself. In fact, Stillman was worried more about the man who'd tried to cop a free feel than he was about Starr, who carried twin derringers in sheaths strapped to her garter belts and wasn't afraid to use them.

Stillman wove Sweets through the traffic and stopped the horse in front of the two, large, open doors of Auld's Livery & Feed Barn, which is where Leon customarily stabled his horse, and which was where he'd likely deposited the bodies he'd ridden into town with. Auld served as the town's liveryman, water-witcher, well digger, gravedigger, wheelwright, and undertaker, which mainly consisted of hammering together simple pine coffins, or wooden overcoats, as Auld called them, and depositing the bodies of the deceased in same. Auld usually hired doxies to bathe and dress the bodies, when such niceties were called for, which wasn't all that often.

Stillman dropped Sweets' reins in the broad

patch of hay-flecked shade fronting the barn and stepped between the doors, peering into the place's deep shadows. "Auld?"

"Ah, Christ! You damn near scared me into a heart stroke, Sheriff!"

Stillman hadn't seen him at first because of the heavy purple shadows, but now as his eyes adjusted from the brassy sunlight, he saw the burly, bearded liveryman in pinstriped overalls and floppy canvas hat standing near an open storage room door about halfway down the barn's central alley. Auld was holding a couple of long pine planks in his arms, and he was scowling at Stillman, red-faced behind his bushy, gray-brown beard that climbed his cheeks to nearly his angry blue eyes.

Beyond him, the barn's rear doors were open. Stillman could see that Auld had the bodies of five men laid out on sheets of plywood propped on sawhorses. Auld's fat tabby cat, Gustave, was sitting on one of the planks, beside one of the dead men. The cat's tail was curled forward around its fat body, and Gustave was blinking slowly and with typical cat-like insouciance as he stared toward his master and Stillman.

"I see Leon made it back with the dead men," Stillman said.

"Ja, he made it back, all right." The liveryman

raised a large, gloved, roast-sized fist threateningly. "And that damned city council better pay me for my work here, because the last time those tight devils made me wait until--"

"I'll see you're paid before you get them cadavers in the ground up on Boot Hill," Stillman said, cutting off the big, beer-bellied German before he could launch himself too deeply in one of his typical tirades. In more civilized places, a coroner's jury would have investigated the deaths, but this far off the beaten path, Stillman unofficially assumed the job as county coroner. In a pinch, a real coroner was brought in from Helena, but only when there was a real question as to the cause of someone's death.

Stillman usually just filled out an affidavit, had it witnessed by Leon or Elmer Burke, who owned the Drovers, and filed it with the circuit judge, who did only God knew what with it . . .

"Do you have the girl, too?" Stillman asked.

"That's what you said last time!"

"I said what last time?"

"That you'd see I was paid promptly but those skinflint devils said they had to wait to see what that crooked banker said about--!"

"Auld!"

"*What?*"

"Do you have the girl back there, too?"

"No, I don't have the girl! I gave your deputy my last wooden overcoat and rented him a buckboard, and he took off for the Triple H Connected! And he didn't pay me one dime for that box! Not one dime! Each box is two dollars, and that barely covers the materials to say nothing about--!"

"Damnit!"

"Damnit is right. You know what I think those city council fellas do with our hard-earned tax money? I think they--!"

"Auld!"

"What?"

"Shut your pie hole and saddle me your fastest mount! Then you can unsaddle Sweets and--!"

"Ben!"

The girl's scream had risen from behind Stillman and back down the street in the direction from which he'd come. The waitress from Sam Wa's Café was running toward him, taking care not to get run over by the horsebackers and farm and ranch wagons hammering up and down the usually quiet street. Fall was always a busy time of the year in Clantick, but the Northern Pacific's push just west of here was making it busier.

Evelyn Vincent was holding the skirts of her cream and salmon Mother Hubbard dress above her black leather shoes, as she gained Stillman's side of the street. Her sandy-blond hair had tumbled half out of the neat chignon she usually wore behind her head when she was working, and her heart-shaped face was red from anxiety.

"What is it, Evelyn?" Stillman asked, walking down the street to meet her.

Just then he heard shouts rising from the far side of the street and down a ways. They seemed to be coming from Sam Wa's place.

"Ben--please, help!" Evelyn cried, grabbing his right wrist and tugging him along behind her. "It's Sam and one of the customers! They're fighting. With knives!"

Stillman started to follow the girl back across the street at a slant, adjusting his big Colt .44 on his left hip and sliding his gaze this way and that, negotiating the traffic. He held his arm out to stop a ranch wagon moving toward him from the left, evoking an indignant bray from one of the mules in the wagon's traces, and then he and Evelyn gained the street's opposite side.

Evelyn was walking slightly ahead of Stillman, nearly running and glancing over her shoulder to say, "He's fighting with one of the customers. The man's a horror. He pulled me onto his lap and kissed me and . . . and he put his hands where . . . well, where no man should put his hands unless he's given permission!" The young blonde paused, breathing hard as she hopped up onto the small, wooden veranda sagging off the front of the small log shack that housed Sam Wa's Café. The smell of fried chicken and steaks and rich gravy mingled with the smell of the blue-tinged wood smoke hovering over and around the shack.

"Wait out here," Stillman told the girl, grabbing her right arm to stop her.

A couple of men dressed in the shabby checked suits of drummers were milling near the front screen door, peering anxiously inside.

"You pay or you go to jail, like everyone else!" Sam Wa was shouting inside the place. His Chinese accent had grown less severe over the several years he'd been living and slinging hash in Clantick. "You pay now and then you go—get the hell out of Sam's place, and never . . .!"

The rotund Chinaman dressed in a purple smock and fringed deerskin trousers over which he wore a soiled, green apron, saw Stillman, and his almond-shaped black eyes brightened. Sam curled a shrewd smile that was framed by his long, gray-brown, mare's tail mustaches that hung several inches down below his lower jaw.

"Sheff, Sheff!" he called, still unable to pronounce "Sheriff" correctly. "Arrest this man. Get him out of here before I gut him like feesh!"

He very easily could have gutted the man with

the large, wooden-handled meat cleaver he was holding in his large, pudgy left fist. Sam and his troublesome customer were both crouched like pugilists in the middle of the restaurant, in a sizeable gap between oilcloth-covered tables.

The customer was Sam's size. He was a sinister-looking cuss with long, coarse, yellow-blond hair hanging past his shoulders, and a thick beard two shades darker than his hair. He wore a ragged buffalo skin vest and checked orange trousers with hide-patched knees, the cuffs stuffed into high-topped, fur-trimmed moccasins. An empty knife sheath jutted from one of the moccasins. The knife was in the man's right hand, and he was holding it up between him and Sam as the two men scuffled around in the gap between the tables, the blonde gent grinning menacingly while Sam was prattling in what Stillman assumed was Chinese.

Stillman had seen the blonde cuss before. He'd been in town a lot recently, drinking and gambling. The sheriff had heard he was a market hunter for the railroad crew working west of here . . . when they weren't in town raising a ruckus, that was.

"Stay out of this, Sheriff!" the blonde gent said, glancing at Stillman and letting his eye flick to the five-pointed star pinned to Stillman's blue, white-pinstriped shirt, near his left brown leather suspender. "This Chinaman's cussin' me out, though he does it in dog-talk so I can't figure it out, but no Chinaman's gonna talk to Seymore M. Scudder that way!"

"Throw those blades down!" Stillman ordered, moving quickly.

"He's nothin' but a damn Chinaman, and he done accused me of not payin' for my meal!" Scudder slashed his big bowie knife at Sam Wa's bulging belly. Sam had been a Chinaman in the American West long enough to have learned how to handle a knife-wielding hooplehead. He expertly feinted, shuffling his slippered feet with uncommon grace while showing his sharp, yellow teeth the way a mountain lion bares its fangs, and growling.

"I gut him, Sheff!" Sam shouted warningly, making slashing motions with blood-crusted meat cleaver. "I gut him now! Sam's gonna carve dis devil up and feed him to my hogs!"

Stillman pushed one of the on-lookers aside. There were five or six men standing around, some placing bets, all yelling encouragement to either Sam or his bearded opponent. Stillman was close enough now he could smell the alcohol stench oozing from Scudder's pores. He was glassy-eyed and stockyard mean from drink.

"Scudder, I told you to throw that knife down!"

The market hunter spun suddenly toward Stillman, pale blue eyes flashing yellow as he said, "Sheriff, if you're sidin' with this heathen, I'll gut you same as him!" He thrust the bowie toward Stillman. The sheriff lurched back just in time to keep himself from being gored by the savagely curled tip of the razor-edged bowie.

Rage burned through Stillman.

He, too, had danced with knife-wielding hoopleheads.

Bounding forward without hesitation, he slammed his right fist into Scudder's face before the hunter could bring the knife back again. Scudder grunted and stumbled backward. Stillman stayed on him, grabbing the blonde market hunter's knife wrist with his own right hand and smashing his left fist into Scudder's face—three quick, brutal jabs that turned the market hunter's nose and lips the deep red of tomato sauce.

As Scudder fell straight backward, screaming and clamping both hands over his ruined face, a man behind Stillman yelled, "I had money on him, you tin-starred son of a buck!"

Stillman wheeled in time to see one of the on-lookers—a barrel-shaped, freckle-faced gent in a rabbit fur hat and rabbit skin vest—begin hauling up a Russian .44 from a holster thonged on his right thigh. Stillman brought his own revolver up first and fired a half-second before the freckle-faced gent's Russian roared.

In the doorway, Evelyn Vincent screamed and clamped her hands over her mouth.

The freckle-faced gent's slug tore into an oil-cloth-covered table several feet to Stillman's left while the shooter twisted around to face the door and dropped his gun as he clamped a hand over the bloody hole in his right arm. He fell to both knees, lifted his head, and spewed hoarse epithets at the ceiling.

He glared, crimson-faced, over his shoulder at the sheriff. "You're gonna die! Oh, Stillman, you're gonna die for that—if it's the last thing I do!"

Stillman sighed and let his pistol hang down along his right thigh. He looked at the man with the ruined face, who was lying supine on the floor, rolling this way and that, clamping his hands to his face and sobbing.

He looked at the barrel-shaped, freckle-faced gent he'd just pinked, and cursed.

If there'd been any doubt before in his ability to leave town, there was none now. Now, he had two prisoners to look after and a wild dog of a town to leash.

His deputy was on his own.

Chapter Five

AS THE BUCKBOARD WAGON crested a steep hill, its iron-shod wheels squawking, Deputy McMannigle drew back on the reins of the rangy piebald in the traces. The horse stopped and shook its head as though sensing the wagon driver's own apprehension.

"What you so edgy about?" Leon griped to the horse. "You didn't shoot the stupid little . . .." He let his voice trail off. He knew better than to speak ill of the dead.

He gave a fateful sigh, poked his hat brim up off his forehead and stared across a creek that ran between hills below him, toward the headquarters of the Triple H Connected Ranch, which sprawled across a tabletop bluff beyond. Cattle grazed along the slope of the bluff, some standing in the creek and staring with dim-witted curiosity up toward McMannigle, water dripping from weeds clinging to their jaws.

A dog's angry barks lured the deputy's gaze up the bluff to where the dog stood under the wooden ranch portal, with the Triple H Connected brand burned into the crossbeam. The dog was a shaggy, tri-color collie or Australian shepherd, and it jerked its snout up with each bark. After every three or four barks it glanced over its left shoulder toward the big house standing on the top of the bluff beyond it, as though looking to see if its warning was being heeded or if it was wasting its time out here.

It was almost dusk. Shadows were growing long and purple with salmon-gold trim.

Purple smoke curled from the large, fieldstone chimney that jutted up from the house's right end. The log house was two and a half stories, and it looked like a barn except for the front porch and the rows of shutter-outfitted windows running along all three stories—and the chimney, of course. A log bunkhouse sat to the left of the house. Two barns of different sizes, several corrals, and sundry outbuildings sat forward and to the right.

McMannigle had been out here twice before with Stillman when Hollister had complained of nesters—small ranchers staking claim to what he considered his own graze. Hollister did not tolerate interlopers of any kind. He'd told the lawmen so when they'd ridden out here. He tolerated neither nesters nor rustlers, and if Stillman and McMannigle didn't deal with the problem, he'd deal with it himself.

With long riatas outfitted with a hangman's noose.

He told the lawmen that much as well. The lawmen knew that Hollister would have preferred to handle the matter himself, and had certainly done so in the past, but was trying to change with these more lawful times.

Now, shaking the reins over the piebald's back and clucking to the horse, starting down the hill, McMannigle wondered how old Hollister would feel about a black man who'd killed his daughter. As he wondered about that, he half-consciously patted his Schofield revolver holstered on his right thigh and glanced at his sheathed Winchester lying under the wagon seat. He'd made sure both weapons were fully loaded, just in case.

Probably crazy, riding out here alone. Not only crazy, he deserved to be fired for it. He'd gone against the wishes of his boss, a man he respected, but something hard and stubborn in the deputy had compelled him to ride out here with the intention of explaining himself. Any man with an ounce of integrity would want to do the same thing. Leon didn't want to hide behind Ben's badge.

What he'd had to do was tragic, but it was justified. If he'd ridden out here with Stillman and let Ben explain it, it might have looked as though something weren't right about what Leon had been forced to do.

The deputy crossed the creek at the bottom of the hill via a stout log bridge, blackbirds cawing in the cattails lining the rippling water that flashed salmon green over white stones. The dog kept barking more and more angrily as the stranger started up the side of the bluff in the wagon. A high, short whistle silenced the dog, who turned and disappeared over the brow of the bluff.

The dog's place was taken by a rider on a brown-and-white pinto pony. The rider held a carbine straight up from his right thigh. He wore a funnel-brimmed Stetson, a sheepskin vest over a brown shirt, and from what Leon could see of his face from a hundred yards away, it looked flat and blandly belligerent. He sat the pinto giving Leon the hairy eyeball as the wagon clattered on up the gradual incline.

The pinto whinnied a greeting, shifting its front hooves, and the skewbald pulling the wagon shook its head and whickered.

As the wagon climbed, the ranch yard spread out in front of McMannigle. It was larger and with more space between buildings than it had appeared from the opposite hill. The main lodge sat back on the far side of the bluff. A tall, lean, gray-haired gent in a dark trousers and suspenders stood on the front veranda.

He appeared to be wearing a bib, and he was chewing. The dog sat beside him, staring intently toward Leon, occasionally shifting its front paws. In the funeral silence now at dusk, the deputy could hear the dog giving soft, throaty mewls and restrained yips.

As McMannigle approached the rider with the rifle, two more men with rifles walked out away from the bunkhouse on the yard's left side. They moved with slow, menacing ease, holding the barrels of their long guns on their shoulders. One was nibbling what appeared a baking powder biscuit.

The deputy had interrupted supper here at the Triple H Connected.

As he halted the wagon in front of the horseback rider, who had canted his head slightly to one side and was giving Leon the stink eye from beneath the brim of his funneled brim hat, which was festooned with a band of small silver conchos, McMannigle saw a curtain move in a lower story window of the house, just right of the half-open door and near the tall, lean, gray-haired gent standing there beside the dog. The lean gent would be Watt Hollister himself.

A pale shape moved in the window in which the curtain had jostled.

The door opened wider behind Hollister and three younger men filed out to stand to the right of the old man but giving themselves a respectful separation from him. They might have been standing slightly farther back on the veranda, as well. Two of roughly the same height were attired in rough range gear, like the waddies now facing and approaching the deputy. The third taller, younger man on the veranda was clad a little more dapperly in gray whipcord trousers, a nice shirt with fancy piping over the shoulders, and a string tie.

He was the oldest boy—Nash Hollister. The other two would be Zebulon and Samuel.

A woman stepped out of the door now as well. This would be Mrs. Hollister. Virginia, Leon believed her name was. She had a dark, knit shawl wrapped over her shoulders; her dark-brown hair coiled in two buns atop her severely shaped head with a pale, oval-shaped face cleaved by a long nose hooked and crooked as an arthritic witch's finger. She'd been the one in the window. She stepped to the opposite side of Hollister from the sons, also giving some separation, and opened the book she held in her hands and started right in, reciting the Lord's Prayer.

There was no doubting what it was. She was reciting it from Good Book loud and clear, not looking down at the book but staring toward the black stranger and the wagon carrying what everyone could probably see was a casket, for the sides of the buckboard were less than a foot high. Her voice rang crisp and clear and without emotion.

". . . Thy will be done in earth, as it in Heaven. Give us this day our daily bread . . ."

"What you got there, boy?" asked the man sitting the pinto twenty feet in front of Leon.

He had a low, raspy voice, and he lifted his spade-shaped chin slightly to indicate the deputy's cargo. McMannigle thought his name was Westin, the foreman. He and the two hands standing to Westin's right regarded Leon with expressions ranging from incredulity to sneering indignation.

McMannigle stared hard at the men facing him, trying to keep his anger on a leash. Now was not a time for anger. He would be treated poorly here, as he usually was by dim-witted white men, but he had a job to do, and the only way to do that job effectively was to remain even-tempered.

That said, he saw no reason to waste time on underlings.

He shook the reins over the skewbald's back and continued forward.

"Hey!" the foreman groused, sharply reining his horse off to Leon's right to avoid being run over.

The skewbald bulled through the space he'd vacated, and the wagon clattered and rattled, and the casket thumped in the box, as the deputy crossed the yard, swerving left around a windmill and stock tank and then pulling up to the lodge's veranda at an angle.

He stopped about fifty feet away. The dog barked once. Hollister looked down at the dog and then tossed the chicken leg he'd been nibbling into the yard, past the woman who was still reciting the Lord's Prayer and holding the open Bible as though for extra comfort. The dog dashed into the yard and attacked the bone as it would a rabbit.

The old man turned to his three sons staring glumly toward the wagon, muttered something McMannigle couldn't hear, then ripped the bib from around his neck, wiped his mouth and walrus mustache with it, and tossed it onto the veranda floor. He moved down the verandah steps and into the yard while the woman continued reciting the Lord's Prayer crisply behind him, staring off into the distance over Leon's right shoulder.

The deputy had recited the words in his head, so he felt he had to say them:

"Mr. Hollister, I'm sorry I have to inform you of this, but there's been an unfortunate turn of events. Last night . . ."

He let his voice trail off. The old man didn't seem to be listening. Watt Hollister moved over to the wagon box and stared grimly down at the simple, pine box that had shifted around a little to sit at an angle in the wagon bed. Leon saw that the lid had popped up slightly on one side though the gap was not wide enough to reveal the coffin's contents.

The old man was stooped over slightly, and broomstick-lean—a gray-headed, gray-mustached scarecrow losing its straw. He appeared as though the simple movement of walking might cause his hips and shoulders to slip from their sockets. His forehead and cheeks, across which his thin, ruddy skin was drawn so taut it appeared as transparent as wax paper, were a mass of liver-colored spots and moles and crimson blemishes.

His sunken, bony jaws and pointed chin resembled a plow blade. His knob-like shoulders were shaking inside his flannel shirt, as was his wing-like arm as he lifted it to set an arthritis-gnarled hand atop the coffin lid.

Leon silently opined that Watt Hollister was not shaking from emotion but from the Palsy.

Staring down at the unvarnished box with a look of heart-rending bereavement, old Hollister said raspily, "My daughter in there?"

"Yessir, she is."

With that, Mrs. Hollister's voice suddenly broke away from the prayer and she raked in an ululating breath. It was a gasp, but it resembled the shrill warbling of a whippoorwill. The woman dropped to her knees with a dull thud. The Bible fell with another thud and a windy flutter of its pages.

Without turning his head, Watt Hollister said quietly, "Zeb, take your mother inside."

The youngest-looking of the Hollister sons moved over to the woman now sobbing with her head down, and gently pulled her to her feet. "Come on, Ma," he said quietly, the breeze playing with his sandy hair that rose to a cowlick in back.

Hollister turned his rheumy brown eyes to Leon and shifted his fragile jaws around as though grinding his teeth, and his long, broad, pitted nose reddened. "How?"

Leon blinked, studied on his answer. He'd been going to tell it just like it had happened. But the old man was so palsied and old and dried up and ready for the grave, that he didn't have the heart to tell it like that. He did not have the heart to tell the truth.

"I shot her by accident," McMannigle said in a low, dull voice, leveling his own gaze on that of the old man glaring back at him. "Sheriff Stillman and I were after rustlers holed up in a cabin on Loco Jack Creek. You probably know the ones I'm talkin' about. They were ..."

"Yeah, I know—they was rustlin' over here in my country. Led up by a young firebrand who used to work fer me. Tommy Dilloughboy. Stinkin' half-breed Injun, Dilloughboy. Cree from Canada. Never shoulda hired his like in the first place. I run him and the others off after my foreman got suspicious. Stretched hemp on two of 'em. I heard they drifted over to the eastern side of the Two-Bears. So, you and Stillman finally caught up to 'em ... and killed my girl in the bargain."

He flared his right nostril at that and continued to grind his jaws around like a milk cow chewing hay.

"That's right, Mr. Hollister. We didn't know she was with those men. They were led by Tommy Dilloughboy, you say?" McMannigle hesitated, wishing that the old man would clarify the girl's presence in the cabin with the rustlers for him.

When no explanation appeared imminent, but the old man only continued to stare at the deputy with red-nosed, smoldering-eyed wrath, Leon cleared his throat and admonished himself to tread carefully. No point in making things worse than they already were. "What I mean to say is-- we didn't know they had her. She was near one of 'em in the cabin, and my bullet, intended for one of the rustlers, struck your daughter."

"You killed her."

"That's right, sir. By accident. And for that, I truly apologize."

"Did you kill all them long-loopers?"

"Yes. Or . . . almost all. One got away but he was wounded. The sheriff went after him, probably found him by now."

Old Hollister sucked another rattling breath and then let his quivering hand flutter atop the coffin lid. Stepping back away from the wagon, he said, "Boys, come on out here and take your sister into the house so we can dress her for a proper burial."

Nash and Samuel Hollister walked down the porch steps and into the yard. Nash was tall and lean like his father, but he was a square-shoul-dered young man. Not so young anymore. He appeared at least thirty. A younger, sturdier ver-sion of the old man. He kept his arrogant, gray-eyed gaze on McMannigle as he led his younger brother, who was a good six inches shorter than Nash, out into the yard.

"The darkie killed her, eh, Pa?" Nash said as though Leon couldn't speak for himself.

The older Hollister just jerked his bony hand, thumb extended, over his shoulder toward the house. "Just haul her in there and keep your damn mouth shut till I tell you to open it!"

Silently, the two brothers slid the coffin out of the wagon and, each taking an end, carried it up the veranda steps and inside the house. The deputy could hear their boots thumping on the floorboards. A shrill cry rose from somewhere inside the house. It rose in volume and began ululating again, like the cry of a bereaved whippoorwill. McMannigle could hear it reverberating in there.

It lifted chicken flesh across his shoulder blades.

Watt Hollister turned to Leon. "You've come a long way. I'd offer you a bait of food, but you'd have to eat it out here. I only allow white folks inside the house. Your badge doesn't mean anything to me."

He'd said it as though without acrimony, as though it were a perfectly reasonable stipulation. That was all right. The deputy had been as casually relegated to the level of vermin before, and far worse. Under the circumstances, he tried not to let it bother him.

"Obliged, but I best be headin' on back to town."

Leon pinched his hat brim to the man and then shook the ribbons over the skewbald's back. He didn't feel obligated to apologize to the man again. He'd done that. He'd even taken sole responsibility for the girl's death. He'd done enough. He was sorry the girl was dead, but his guilt was assuaged.

He was sorry he'd had to go against Ben's orders, but he was glad he'd come.

Hearing the woman's squeals in the house behind him, and the dog's half-hearted barks, the deputy aimed the wagon for the portal at the edge of the yard. The horseback rider with the funnel-brimmed hat was still sitting his pinto there, the horse's white spots glowing in the darkness.

The other three men with rifles were lined out beside Westin, standing slackly, thumbs in their pockets, heads canted to one side. It had gotten darker since Leon had ridden into the yard, and the men were standing in menacing silhouette against the cloud-scalloped, salmon-streaked western sky. More men were standing around outside the lamplit windows of the bunkhouse. Smoke from their cigarettes or cigars wafted grayly in the purple shadows.

None of the punchers said anything as Leon put the horse and wagon under the portal and started on down the hill toward Clantick.

The old man walked a little unsteadily across the verandah and into the house. The dog was behind him, mewling.

Nash was waiting in the kitchen lit by a bracket lamp, leaning his big frame against one wall near a loudly ticking grandfather clock. Hollister's oldest was smoking a cigarette.

The old man stopped just inside the door and turned to stare back outside at where the wagon was a fading gray blur in the darkness at the edge of the yard. Its clattering was drowned by the howling of Virginia from upstairs, where the boys had deposited the coffin of their dead sister in her room.

"I don't want that man to make it back to town, Nash."

The son chuckled softly, incredulously. "You sure, Pa? He is a lawman. Stillman's deputy. You sure you wanna go up against Still--?"

"You heard me," the old man said, so low and brittle as to be nearly inaudible. "I want him dead. I don't want there to be any sign of him. The man, the horse, the wagon—I don't want anyone to find them. I don't want a trace of that man to ever be found." He glanced over his shoulder. "You hear me? He killed your sister. A black man. I want it like he was never even alive."

Nash stared at the old man, blinked once slowly, sighed, and shrugged his left stout shoulder. "All right."

"Wait till he's off the Triple H Connected and then get rid of him. I don't want him goin' back to Clantick and talkin' about your sister."

"All right, Pa," Nash said, brushing past the frail old man and casually strolling outside, blowing cigarette smoke out his nostrils. "It ain't gonna change what become of Orlean, but I reckon you're the boss."

Chapter Six

"GIVE NO QUARTER," Sam Wa was saying now at the end of the night in the kitchen of his restaurant. "Give no quarter to rabid dogs or men who don't pay!" He slapped a pudgy hand down on the food preparation table before him. "Ha! No quarter to rabid dogs or men who don't pay!"

Sam sat at the stout, scarred wooden table, sitting back in his chair with a sharp-eyed look, puffing his opium pipe, which was the fanciest pipe Evelyn Vincent had ever seen, carved as it was with tiny green dragons spewing red flames down the pipe's stem to the broad, porcelain bowl.

It was midnight and they'd finally closed. They'd finished cleaning up, and Evelyn was pouring a wooden bucket containing the last of the night's food scraps—steak bones, bread crusts, egg shells, coffee grounds, leftover potatoes, and rice and whatnot--into a large, corrugated tin tub.

"That's right, Sam," she said, straightening and blowing a vagrant lock of sandy blond hair from her blue right eye. "Give no quarter!"

"Give no quarter. Ha!"

"That's right—give no quarter to men who don't pay."

"No quarter. That means when they don't pay I do just what I did today—I take a cleaver after them." The round-faced Chinamen laughed around the pipestem, puffing the cloying, sweet-smelling smoke into the air of the kitchen still rife with the smell of cooked food and scorched lard and steak grease. "Did you see me with the cleaver, Evan?" While his English was pretty good, there were some names, including hers, he could not pronounce.

"I saw you and your cleaver, Sam." Evelyn said, dragging the big tin washtub over to the kitchen's rear door that faced the alley behind the café as well as Sam's little log shanty and his hog pen and chicken coop. "I just wish I would have seen both of you a little earlier, when that drunken renegade was grabbing me in places respectable men just don't grab respectable young women. Without permission, that is!"

Evelyn was thinking that she wouldn't mind

being grabbed in those places by someone nice, someone she liked. She was well into her twenties, and it was about time she was grabbed like that again. It had been awhile since the last time. At least, it had been awhile since the last time she'd been grabbed and touched and fondled by someone she was fond of. Since she'd been gently kissed. If she wasn't careful, she was going to end up an old maid emptying Sam Wa's slop buckets while the pie-eyed Chinaman sat back in his chair getting loopy on that pretty pipe of his when she was ninety years old—all stooped over and pinched-face, dried up, and mean from lack of love in her life.

Doc Evans's intellectually handsome face passed across her mind's eye, and she physically shook it away. That was silly. She had to admit feeling an attraction to the man, but he was a good fifteen years older than she, much better educated—why he'd probably read nearly every book that had been written since the Bible—and, besides, he was spoken for. Sometime soon, he'd marry his sometimes helper, Katherine Kemmett, who, traveling clear across Hill County as a nursemaid and midwife, had similar interests to the Doc's. Everyone in town knew the two were meant for each other and would soon be married though Evelyn didn't think they'd set a date yet.

The doc, a bachelor for so long, was dragging his feet on the matter. That's why, Evelyn supposed, she still held out a glimmer of hope that maybe . . .

She chuffed at her silliness and, pulling on her striped wool blanket coat, returned her attention to Sam Wa. "Like I was sayin', I'd appreciate it, Sam, if you and your meat cleaver would . . ."

Evelyn let her voice trail off, turning her mouth corners down. There was no point. Sam was staring dreamily through the heavy smoke wafting around his head, his black eyes reflecting the light of the Rochester light hanging over the table before him. He was busy reliving his prowess with the meat cleaver and his admirable unwillingness to give quarter to men who don't pay their bills.

Despite that it was thanks to Ben Stillman's intervention that he didn't end up getting himself gutted like a fish, Evelyn thought with an inward chuckle as she opened the door and dragged the heavy washtub outside into the dark, windy alley. She dragged the tub over to the wooden wheelbarrow, looked down at the slop-filled tub, and then moved back over to the door and poked her head inside.

"Hey, Sam, how 'bout . . .?"

Sam was holding the cleaver up in front of

his chin and chuckling through his long, yellow teeth as he flicked his thumb across the blade, thoroughly smitten with himself. Evelyn knew by the pulsating, yellow light in the man's muddy eyes that he was lost in an opium fog. Soon, he'd amble over to his cabin—if he didn't fall asleep on a straw pallet he kept in his office part of the café kitchen, that was—and be sound asleep until an hour after Evelyn had returned in the morning to start serving breakfast.

Evelyn gave a disgusted chuff and closed the door. She went over to the tub and had little trouble wrestling it onto the wheelbarrow. She'd wrestled that tub onto the wheelbarrow twice a day for the past two years that she'd been working for Sam. Evelyn wasn't a big girl, but the backs of her thighs and her arms and her back were strong. She'd make a good wife one day; Sam had told her when he'd come upon her making the maneuver.

"Fat chance," Evelyn said now as the cool, autumn breeze spiced with the smell of wood fires blew her hair around her face.

She grabbed the barrow's handles and gave a grunt as she began pushing it along the well-worn path behind the café. She curved around Sam's stone and wood keeper shed and root cellar and the privy then crossed a trash-strewn lot to where Sam's shake-shingled cabin sat amongst several cottonwood trees and lilac bushes, all of which now had nearly finished shedding their leaves.

She pushed the wheelbarrow and the stinky washtub around behind Sam's shack, dark and silent in the cool, breezy, starry night, and over to the shed and large stable. To the right of the stable were Sam's chickens, which Evelyn had locked up in their coop several hours ago, so a weasel or mink wouldn't slip through the chicken wire fence and go on a slaughtering tear. Sam relied on his chickens, just as he did his hogs, over at the café. One of his specialties was chicken and dumplings. Another was well-seasoned pork chops, and his bacon was regarded as second to none on the Hi-Line.

Evelyn aimed the wheelbarrow for the hog pen that sat on the stable's left side. Behind the hog pen and the chicken coop was the paddock housing Sam's mule.

In the corner of Evelyn's left eye, a shadow moved.

Evelyn gasped as she stopped pushing the wheelbarrow and released the handles. "Who's there?"

She stared toward the back of Sam's leaning shack. Starlight limned the spidery shrubs that abutted the stone foundation, near a large pile of logs that Sam would hire one of the town's odd-job men, likely Olaf Weisinger, to split for him before the first snow flew.

Evelyn could pick out nothing but the breeze-jostled shrubs and the firewood.

"Is someone there?" she called, lifting her hand to slide a lock of wayward hair behind her left eye.

Her heart thudded. She'd seen something move over there, near Sam's shack. But now she could see nothing but the shack itself and the bushes. She must have only seen the movement of the bushes in the breeze. Or perhaps one of the town's many stray cats had leaped down from Sam's low roof and scuttled off in the brush.

It was dark out here, and the only sound was the breeze, though in the distance she could hear the hammering of a piano in one of the saloons. She recognized the playing of Merle Stroud, a retired cowboy who played at the Drovers every weekend. This was Friday night. Or Saturday morning, more like. Folks were having fun. At least, it seemed everyone was having fun except poor, lonely, over-worked Evelyn Vincent.

She had no family. No beau. Few friends. She had to work so darn much to keep herself fed and housed over at Ma Latham's boarding house that she didn't have time for friends. The chicken flesh that had risen all up and down Evelyn's back retreated. Now it was replaced by the hollow ache of loneliness and the nagging disenchantment of a young woman's stymied life. The distant patter of the piano and the occasional whooping and hollering of Friday night revelers mocked her.

"Oh, hell," she said, sort of enjoying the raw ache of self-pity. A girl had a right to indulge herself now and then.

Slumped like a martyr, she continued pushing the wheelbarrow over to where Sam's half-dozen hogs slumbered in piles of straw beneath the stable's overhang. She wrinkled her nose against the fetor, and then lifted the wash bucket by the handles on each end and heaved it over the top rail with a grunt.

Splat!

A couple of the hogs heard and smelled the fresh delivery and grunted as they climbed to their feet and came thumping over, hanging their heads low to the ground and oinking hungrily.

"Enjoy, boys," Evelyn said.

She'd just started to turn back to the wheelbarrow when she heard the crunch of footsteps in the coarse weeds and gravel behind her. An arm was thrust around her head from behind and a large, rough hand closed over her mouth, muffling Evelyn's startled yelp.

The hand pulled her back against a man's rising and falling chest—she could feel the desperate heat of him behind her—and then she saw a face slide up close to her right cheek. It was a dark, ruddy face framed with thick, dark hair.

"*Shhh!* Evelyn, don't scream, okay? It's me, Tommy. Tommy Dilloughboy!"

That froze her. She slid her eyes far to the right. Sure enough, it was Tommy. She could see his dark-tan, handsome, brown-eyed face in the darkness.

Slowly, he took his hand away, holding it up in front of her face for a few seconds, in case he should need it again. Then, when she didn't scream but only continued to stare at him in wide-eyed surprise, he grinned, showing all his solid, white teeth including the front one that was chipped a little and which somehow only added to the young man's boyish handsomeness. Tommy's thick, wavy hair blew around beneath his hat in the breeze.

"Tommy, what are you doing here?" Evelyn said.

"Shh," he said, placing a finger against his full, well-formed lips. He smiled again to put her at ease, his cheeks dimpling. "Don't exactly wanna advertise the fact. It bein' so late and all, I mean. Might wake the neighbors."

"I thought you were working out at the Triple H Connected," Evelyn said, keeping her voice down.

"Yeah, well, I was, but . . . you know, after roundup, over half the crew got cut. I reckon you could say I'm sorta ridin' the grubline." Tommy grinned and wrapped his arms around her. "Sure is good seein' you again, Evelyn. I swear, I was thinkin' about you all summer till I was fit to be tied. I wasn't all that unhappy when old Hollister cut me." He pulled her closer, held her tighter. "Gave me the chance to come callin' on you, see your purty eyes again."

"Oh, Tommy." Evelyn gazed up at him, slid a lock of hair away from his right eye.

It had been several months since she'd last seen him after they'd spent four blissful weeks in the spring, riding in the country together and taking walks around town and along the river. They'd first met at Sam Wa's, and he'd asked her out the very first time they spoke. She hardly knew the boy, but Evelyn had found herself pining for him to distraction after he'd had to leave and accept a summer job, punching cattle out at the Hollister ranch.

He'd gotten into some trouble in town. Nothing serious. Just the usual stuff hot-blooded young men get into, and that had been another reason he'd felt the need to leave town for a while. To give Sheriff Stillman and Deputy McMannigle time to forget about him.

"You come back to town to find work?" Evelyn asked him, still gazing up at those big, round eyes of his. She swore that Tommy Dilloughboy was like peppermint candy that melted in a girl's mouth the second it touched her tongue.

"Well sorta. And . . . well, I sorta got a problem, Evelyn."

"What is it, Tommy? What happened?"

The young man winced, grunted. He placed his hand on his side. There was a bulge beneath his shirt. Over the bulge the young man's blue-and-red plaid shirt glistened faintly in the starlight. Evelyn gently placed her hand over the bandage, felt the cool, oily substance soaking his shirt and which could only be blood oozing from a wound in his side.

Evelyn sucked a sharp breath. "Oh, Tommy!"

Chapter Seven

LEON MCMANNIGLE HAULED back on the skewbald's reins.

The wagon clattered to a stop on the pale two-track trail curling through a shallow canyon somewhere west of the Triple H Connected. The horse blew, breath frosting in the cool night air.

The deputy turned to look over his right shoulder, narrowing his eyes to probe the darkness along his back trail.

"What the hell was that?" he muttered.

He'd heard something. He wasn't sure what that something was. Possibly a shod hoof ringing off a stone. About fifty yards back he'd had to swing the wagon around rocks that had apparently rolled down from the low but steep, southern ridge to litter the trail. If he had horseback riders following him, one of their horses might have kicked one of those stones.

Leon stared along his night-cloaked back trail. The southern ridge was steeper than the northern one, and it was butterscotch colored in the darkness. The northern ridge was darker with foliage, piñon and ponderosa pines and Douglas firs climbing the gentler but higher ridge toward the star-shot sky. Now as McMannigle stared up that long, dark ridge stretching toward the firmament, there was a soft, muffled thud, like that of a pinecone tumbling to the ground. At least, that's what it had sounded like.

Could have been a footfall. There was another sound on its heels. A man's grunt?

Apprehension tightened the muscles across the lawman's back.

Were men up there?

Leon hadn't liked the way his visit to the Hollister place had gone. Of course, he hadn't expected the old man to shake his hand and invite him inside for a glass of brandy and a Havana cigar. But he hadn't expected such menace, either. The old man had not been openly hostile, but his eyes set deep in leathery sockets had fairly glowed with fury when he'd learned that his daughter had been residing in Auld's wooden overcoat.

Had that fury compelled Watt Hollister to send his men after McMannigle?

Could the old rancher be so incensed by his

daughter's death that he'd actually try to murder the lawman who'd killed her?

Leon vaguely wished he had gone ahead and told the old man the truth: That the little fool had had that bullet coming to her. Maybe that would have clarified things for old Hollister, made the old man realize the shooting really hadn't been McMannigle's fault at all. It had been Miss Orleans's fault entirely.

Hollister's sending men after him would be what the deputy deserved for trying to soften to the old man's blow. A mistake, he'd told him. An errant shot. McMannigle's ass it was!

Leon looked around. Suddenly, the night was quiet. No more hoof thuds, no more falling pinecones or grunts. Maybe his imagination had been playing tricks on him. Maybe no men were skulking around behind and around him, after all. Old Hollister was a respected Hi-Line rancher. Yeah, he was known to hire cold steel artists to protect his land and his herds from interlopers and long-loopers, but most ranchers did that, especially those operating as remotely as Hollister was.

Mostly—at least as far as Leon knew, and aside from hanging a rustler now and then--the old man and his boys were law-abiding citizens. True, they were obviously broken up by the death of their daughter and sister, but they wouldn't be stupid or criminal enough to try to kill the deputy county sheriff who'd shot her and taken responsibility for it.

Would they?

No. Leon's imagination had gotten away from him, that's all. None of the Hollisters were cold-blooded murderers.

Feeling a little easier, Leon looked around again but this time in hopes of finding a place to camp for the night. He shivered inside his plaid wool coat and lifted the fleece-lined collar against the chill. Damn cold out here. Had to be below freezing. There was no moon, so it was good and dark. The stars helped a little, but Mc-Mannigle didn't want the skewbald to trip over a rock like those behind him and fall and break a leg or even just throw a shoe. They were still a good two, maybe three hours from Clantick, and he didn't want to get stranded way out here afoot. Ranches out this way were literally few and far between. He wouldn't find help for days.

He needed a protected place somewhere off the trail a ways. Not seeing what he wanted anywhere near, he clucked the skewbald ahead. The wagon rattled and barked along the canyon trail. The din it was lifting caused Leon to grind his teeth. If there was anyone stalking him, they'd have no trouble finding him, with all the noise the wagon was making.

He crossed a low divide and dropped into another, broader valley. A stream prattled along the base of the high, forested slope on his right. He spotted a horseshoe clearing in the forest that ran down onto the valley floor, and turned the skewbald off the trail, drawing up to the edge of the clearing a minute later. He inspected the prospective bivouac, deeming it suitable, and then parked the wagon against the west side of the notch forming the clearing, which was backed up by the forested slope and the creek.

Leon thought the creek was one of several forks of Cavalry Creek, so named for a Cavalry patrol ambushed here by Crow Indians a dozen years ago. Here at the west side of the clearing, the wagon would be somewhat concealed by the shadow of a steep escarpment to the west, which sprouted like a large, gray flower from the top of the gradual, forested slope, blotting out a small portion of the stars.

Quickly, McMannigle unharnessed and tended the horse, picketing the tired beast to a pine near the rippling water. He rubbed the horse down with a scrap of burlap, fed it a bait of oats from a feed sack he'd outfitted the wagon with, and then gathered wood.

Soon, he had a small fire dancing and smoking in a pit he'd dug near the stream. It was in a low point of the clearing, but he did not delude himself into thinking the flames could not be seen from the main trail only a couple of hundred yards to the north. If it had been warmer under similar circumstances he would have cold-camped, but it was too damn cold to camp out here without a fire, especially since he doubted Hollister was on his trail.

The more he thought about it, the more absurd it seemed. Hollister had not lived to push seventy years old, having built up a prosperous cattle ranch—one of the most prosperous not only in the Two-Bears but in northern Montana Territory, in fact—to turn killer late in life. He might be madder'n an old wet hen, and he might be grieving the loss of his daughter, but he was not a killer.

Just the same, Leon kept his Winchester carbine near as he brewed a pot of Arbuckles and nibbled the deer jerky and biscuits he'd shoved into his saddlebags before he'd lit out from Clantick. While the coffee brewed, he spread his hot roll near a grassy thumb of turf that, in lieu of his saddle, which he had not brought, would have to serve as a pillow.

He hauled his makings sack out of his coat

pocket and rolled a smoke. By the time he'd sealed the quirley, his coffee water was boiling, so he added a small handful from his Arbuckles pouch, gave the water a minute to return to a boil, removed it from the fire, and added a little cool water from his canteen, which he'd filled from the creek, to settle the grounds.

He poured the hot, black brew into his old, battered, speckled-black tin cup that he'd been using in camps since he'd been a buffalo soldier, fighting the Apaches down in the Southwest just after the War Between the States. The cup was half-rusted where it was badly dented, and the handle was loose, but the cup and the man had been through too much together for the man to cast the storied, old vessel aside just yet.

The cup was beaten up, but it still held coffee. Even kept it hot on cold nights like this one here. It was an old, familiar companion when no other friends were near.

The cup smoking beautifully, tendrils of steam curling toward the stars, McMannigle sat back against a rock near the fire. He'd intended to smoke and drink the coffee leisurely, taking his time and enjoying himself, but his keen ears had been picking up muffled sounds since just after he'd started to roll the quirley, before his coffee pot had started boiling, dribbling water down its spout. It hadn't been easy, rolling the quirley as though nothing were bothering him, but his experience in Apacheria had taught him to remain calm when the chips were down.

To be patient.

Someone—at least five but maybe six or even seven men—were trying to sneak around him in the darkness. His imagination had not been playing tricks on him after all. They could be your average owlhoots looking to rob a lone rider of his horse and guns and anything else they could find of value on his person, but he didn't think so.

He was beginning to think his initial apprehension about old Watt Hollister had been right, after all.

The horse whickered softly. It was an older horse, its senses dull, or it likely would have picked up the stalkers earlier. Now, even, it looked around only briefly before lowering its head to crop the buffalo grass growing around the aspens lining the creek.

Leon's ears were pricked, listening intently. It was hard to pick out the sounds of furtive footsteps above the chuckling of the creek, but he could do it. He could hear the occasional crunch of grass and the muffled snap of a small twig. Meanwhile, shifting his eyes from side to side while keeping his head pointed at the fire without moving it overmuch, he pretended to casually enjoy his coffee and his cigarette. Inside his chest, his heart was beating slowly but heavily, like a war drum during a powwow the night before an attack.

Leon feigned a yawn, blew cigarette smoke into the darkness to his left, using the opportunity to scan the slope rising not ten feet away from him. The horse was on that side but behind him, the wagon on that side, as well, but several yards in front of him. Now, as he began to turn his head back forward, he saw a shadow slip out of the trees about twenty feet up the slope.

He held his head forward and continued to sip his coffee and smoke the quirley. As he did, he watched the stalker on the slope out the corner of his left eye. Meanwhile, men were moving toward him from both sides of the horseshoe-shaped clearing. He could see their shadows. At times, he could even see starlight winking off the rifles they were carrying.

Hastily counting the shadows, he came up with seven men, including the gent now crabbing toward him down the slope.

As long as the man was moving, Leon would hold his position.

In the corner of his left eye, the man stopped. McMannigle saw him raise a rifle. The deputy slung his coffee cup away, and, tucking the quirley into a corner of his mouth, he grabbed his carbine and threw himself sharply left as the rifle of the stalker on the western rise flashed and cracked. The slung plunked into the deputy's nearly full coffee pot, and spilled coffee sizzled and steamed on the leaping flames, smelling like pine tar.

Leon rolled and rose to one knee, cocking and raising his carbine to his shoulder, quickly aiming and firing.

The man on the slope gave a high-pitched screech, dropping his rifle and making a face as he grabbed his left knee with both hands.

The wounded shooter screamed again, "I'm *hit!*" and lost his footing. He rolled down the slope to pile up at the base of it, writhing and yelping like a gut-shot coyote. "I'm hit! I'm hit! Oh, god, I'm hit!"

A brief glimpse at the sandy-haired kid in a blue wool coat clutching his bloody knee and writhing at the edge of the firelight told Leon he'd just shattered the knee of Hollister's youngest, Zebulon.

The skewbald loosed a shrill whinny, bucking and pulling at its tether rope.

Rifles began barking in the darkness of the clearing, red-blue flames lashing toward Leon, who dropped again and rolled and came up running wildly, splashing across Cavalry Creek and desperately climbing the slope into the pines while men shouted and rifles barked and bullets chewed into the slope at his heels and into the trees around him--tearing the night wide open at its seams.

Chapter Eight

_____

"WHOA," SAID TOMMY Three-Hawks, stumbling into Evelyn's arms.

"Tommy!"

"Shhh," Tommy said. "No one'd best know I'm in town, Evelyn. Stillman finds out . . . sees me with a bullet hole . . . he's liable to come to the wrong conclusion. An understandable conclusion, given my less than respectable history here in Clantick, but the wrong conclusion just the same."

Evelyn couldn't hold him. He slipped out of her grasp and dropped to one knee, groaning and clamping a hand over the blood staining the left side of his shirt, a few inches above his cartridge belt.

"Tommy, don't die," Evelyn said, dropping to a knee beside him and staring anxiously into his handsome face. She'd thought she'd forgotten about him but now, seeing him again—especially seeing him again injured—made her realize that she'd only been suppressing thoughts about the wild, handsome young half-breed with the devil-may-care-glint in his dark-brown eyes.

He drew a raking breath, swallowed, winced, and shook his head. "Ah, it's only a flesh wound."

"We gotta get you to Doc Evans."

"No!"

"No? Tommy, you need a doctor. Only Doc Evans can get that bullet out of your side!"

"The bullet ain't in there. It just pinched my side's all. I just need to get it cleaned out, need a place I can lie down for a spell. Sleep. Maybe get some vittles down my throat."

Evelyn slid his hair back from the side of his face and touched his left cheek and forehead. His skinny was sweat-beaded, clammy. "Tommy, you're burnin' up!"

He looked at her desperately. "Really, Evelyn—I just need a place I can hole up for a day or two. You must know a place, don't you? Nobody knows this town like you do."

Evelyn gazed at him skeptically. What was he up to?

"Tommy, how did this happen?"

He turned his head away, spat in disgust. "Ah, hell—you won't believe me if I told you."

Irritation spiked through the young woman. She straightened and stepped back away from the handsome firebrand, crossing her arms on her chest. "Tommy Dilloughboy, if you expect me to help you, you'd better be straight-up with me!"

"Eveylyn, *shhhh!*"

Raising her hard-edged voice, she said, "And you can stop shushin' me right now! Are you playin' me for a fool? You know what I think? I think you got yourself into trouble again, threw in with the wrong curly wolves just like you did last summer, and got shot holding up a bank or a stage coach."

Tommy stared up at her, his eyes wide and round with exasperation. Gradually, he turned his mouth corners down and looked away from her. "Ah, hell—I can't blame you for believin' that. Not after what happened last summer."

He'd thrown in with two other young men and raised hell in a couple of the saloons in Clantick and over in Big Sandy. Considering themselves the next James gang, Evelyn supposed, they'd concocted a plan to rob the Drovers Saloon in broad daylight. Thank goodness the liveryman, Emil Auld, had overheard them talking behind his barn one morning and informed Ben Stillman.

Ben had intervened before the trio of would-be tough nuts could follow through with their devious scheme and ruin the whole rest of their lives. The sheriff had thrown Tommy and his cohorts into jail for a week, so they could take stock and reconsider the path their lives were taking. Only when they'd promised to follow the straight-and-narrow from then on as well as vowed to not show themselves in Clantick for the next year, Ben released them.

That was the last that Evelyn had seen of Tommy until now.

"Of course you can't blame me for believing that," Evelyn said. "My old man always said a zebra can't change his stripes."

"Ah, come on, Evelyn. I ain't no zebra. And I ain't no curly wolf, neither."

"What are you, then? How did you get yourself shot?"

He gazed up at her, his dark eyes even rounder than before. Those eyes and those looks he gave her sent a warm hand sliding down her belly and made it hard for her to keep her dander up. But she would, by god, until she was sure he'd told her the truth about his current situation.

Evelyn Vincent might be many things, but she would not allow a boy to make a fool of her more than once!

She kept her gaze hard and uncompromising,

her face set grimly, skeptically, as she stared down at the young man where he knelt before her, the starlight flashing in his liquid-brown eyes.

"I didn't get myself shot," he said, sheepishly indignant. "Someone took a pot shot at me after I'd left Triple H Connected. I was headin' over to the Chinook country, hopin' to get more ranch work or maybe livery barn work for the winter. Bad luck was doggin' my heels, I reckon. Just like it's done my whole doggone life. Some no-account I never even seen was out to rob me. He or they—I don't even know how many there were--popped this here pill at me, knocked me out of my saddle. I hit my head on a rock. Must've been unconscious for a time, because when I woke up my horse and everything I owned except my coat and my gun was gone! I got to town by hitchin' a ride in a freight wagon."

He stared up at her, grimly.

Evelyn stared down at him.

"Ah, hell." He turned his head away from her head and punched the ground with the edge of his fist. "Ouch!" He shook his fist. "Don't worry about it. If someone like me told me such a sad tale, I wouldn't believe him anymore than you believe me." He sucked a deep breath and heaved himself unsteadily to his feet. "That's all right, Evelyn. I just thought . . . I just thought after what we meant to each other for a time last spring . . ."

"Tommy, where you going?"

He kept walking off along the rear of Sam's stable, heading away from her. The breeze tussled his thick, brown hair, lifted the hem of his ratty blanket coat to reveal the gun and holster strapped around his right leg. Glancing over his right shoulder, wincing, he said, "Not sure yet. I'll find a place. I'll be all right, Evelyn. I'm sorry to pester you. Good night."

She'd already run over and grabbed his left arm, stopping him. "Tommy, don't be ridiculous. You can't just wander off on this dark and cold night with that hole in your side oozing blood like it is."

"There's probably an old abandoned trapper's or prospector's cabin down by the river I can hole up in."

"But you won't have any wood, and you're in no condition to gather any. Tommy, won't you please let me take you to Doc Evans?"

"He'll just tell ole Stillman. You heard the sheriff. He didn't want to see me in town for a year. He sees me, he'll throw me in the calaboose again, and I ain't goin' back to his calaboose."

"Doc Evans won't tell Ben."

"Sure he will."

Evelyn shook her head. "No, he won't. Not if I ask him not to. The doc's a good friend of mine."

Tommy cocked a brow. "How good?"

"Oh, stop it! Can you ride a little ways?"

Clamping a hand over his lower left side, the young man stretched his lips back from his teeth. "Not far. I reckon I could ride as far as Evans's place, though, if I had to."

"Well, you have to. You're burnin' up and you've lost a lot of blood. You need a doctor, and Doc Evans is the best. Wait here!"

Evelyn ran around behind the hog pen and into the paddock housing Sam Wa's mule, whom Sam had not named but whom Evelyn called Whiskers because of his brushy muzzle. The mule brayed with a start when he saw Evelyn and backed away. Recognizing the girl's familiar face, however, he thrashed his tail from side to side, gave a stomp of his front hoof in eager greeting, and brayed again.

"Oh, hush, Whiskers," Evelyn admonished the beast though she figured that Sam was deep in his opium cups by now and wasn't hearing a thing but only chopping up the kitchen table with his meat cleaver and seeing the face of the man who'd refused to pay his bill.

When Evelyn had wrestled a hackamore over Whiskers' ears, she led the docile mule around to the front of the stable, where Tommy was sitting on the ground, his back to the stable door. His head hung forward, as though he were half asleep.

Evelyn's voice roused him, and he grinned. "For a minute there, I thought you'd run off on me."

"You know I wouldn't do that," Evelyn said in mock disgust, her brusque tone belying the good feeling that had come over her, encountering the charming young half-breed again while the sensible part of her admonished her to tread carefully. Maybe it was just plain old female instinct, but she felt a warm self-satisfaction in being needed. Especially by a young man she realized she was still very much charmed by, if not in love with, which was possible.

How quickly her dour mood and dark outlook had lightened and colored, her loneliness retreated, in only the past ten minutes.

"Can you climb up onto Whiskers' back, Tommy? He's a big son of a buck!"

She helped the young man to his feet.

"I'll make it."

They each used the overturned slop bucket as a step and swung up onto the mule's back; Evelyn first and then Tommy seated himself behind her.

"Don't worry, Tommy," Evelyn said into the breeze, which blew her badly mussed hair back behind her shoulders. "Doc Evans will have you back on your feet in no time."

She batted her heels against the mule's flanks.

Whiskers brayed and lunged into a trot, heading down an alley that paralleled Clantick's main street, in the direction of Clyde Evans' big, old house perched on a butte on the town's western edge.

~~~

"Nash!"

"Zeb!'

"Help me, Nash! Samuel! Oh, Christ—I'm hit bad!"

Nash Hollister stared over the top of his covering boulder and saw the deputy run up the slope beyond the fire and the creek and disappear in the darkness. The man's horse had broken free of its picket rope and was now galloping off across the clearing, buck-kicking angrily at the fusillade. A couple of the other Triple H Connected men were shooting toward the slope, rifles cracking, powder smoke wafting in the cool air.

"Hold your fire! Hold your fire!" Nash shouted, holding up his left hand. "Don't waste your bullets!"

Nash looked at his youngest brother, Zebulon, writhing on his back to the right of the deputy's fire that was still steaming from the spilled coffee. The middle Hollister brother, Samuel, was hunkered behind the rock to Nash's right.

"Zeb, hold on—we're comin' for ya!" Samuel looked at Nash. "Holy Christ—its sounds like he's hit bad." His voice had a frightened tremor in it. His long, gray eyes—the same shape and color as their mother's—sparked with worry. Samuel was the weakest of the three brothers. The laziest and the weakest, and he was also the worrier in the family. Tears glistened in his eyes now and began to dribble down his cheeks, resembling small, gold beads in the firelight. "What're we just sittin' here for? Zeb's hurt bad, Nash!"

Nash was aiming his rifle at the slope. His voice was low, raspy. "All right. You go. I'll cover you. Wouldn't put it past the darkie to lay in wait for us up there to get lit by his fire. Go, but be careful, Samuel. Keep your head about your fool self!"

Samuel was up and running, holding his rifle low in his left hand, not even looking toward the slope. "I'm comin', Zeb! Hold on, little brother!"

"Ah, hell—I'm hit bad, Samuel!" Zebulon cried, his voice so pinched now as to be almost inaudible.

Nash scrutinized the slope. The fire was dying. That was good. It meant the deputy couldn't see them much better than Nash and his men could see him. Deciding the man had probably run on up the slope—he wasn't fool enough to try to take on six men armed with rifles, men who also had horses when he himself was on foot—Nash slowly rose from behind his rock. Holding his rifle at port arms across his chest, he moved over to where Samuel was kneeling beside the writhing, bawling Zeb, but he kept his eyes on the slope.

"How is he?"

"Ah, Christ, Nash—look at his knee!"

"Devil done crippled me, Nash!" Zeb sobbed. "Kill his black ass for me!"

Nash glanced at Zeb's knee, which was all blood. It looked as though the younker had taken the bullet in the kneecap, shattering it.

"Get him up." Nash glanced at the four other men, who were sort of crouching over their aimed rifles and staring warily up the slope beyond the fire. "You fellas get after him! I gotta get Zeb back to the ranch. He's hurt bad. You stay after that damn tin star and finish him—hear? There'll be a bonus in it for you."

The four were not the best of Nash's lot because he hadn't thought he'd need his best for one lone lawman in a wagon. The fewer involved in this, the better. The fair to middling rawhiders glanced around at each other, silently conferring. Meanwhile, Samuel had wrapped one of Zeb's arms around his neck and was hoisting the howling young man to his feet.

"What is it?" Nash asked the four gunmen whom he and his father had hired to keep nesters off the sprawling Triple H Connected range.

The rawhider who called himself Morgan swallowed, his Adam's apple rising and falling in his long, unshaven neck in the firelight. "It's dark. And he has the high ground. Might be best if we wait till mornin'."

The other three flanking Morgan looked at Nash expectantly, seeming to agree with their spokesman.

"You wait till mornin', you can kiss that bonus good-bye. And you can haul your freight off the Triple H Connected, for all that. Good luck tryin' to find more work this late in the year."

The four glanced around at each other again darkly. Morgan shrugged. Turning their mouth corners down, they moved around the fire, spread out, crossed the creek, and began climbing the slope, staying about fifteen feet apart. They moved slowly, crouching, aiming their rifles up at the dark columns of the pines above the deputy's bivouac.

Nash helped Samuel get the sobbing, groaning, often-mewling young Zeb started back to where they'd tied their horses. They hadn't gone more than ten feet before a man shouted, "There!"

A rifle cracked loudly. The slug spang shrilly.

Another rifle farther up the slope thundered and flashed amidst the gauzy pines. It kept thumping and flashing, the shots echoing hoarsely around the valley and nearly drowning out the screams of the four rawhiders whom Nash had turned around to watch roll wildly back down the slope through the pines.

They flung away their rifles and lost their hats. Their spurs chimed raucously. One rolled all the way down the slope to splash into the shallow creek beyond the fire.

The rifle fell silent.

The man in the creek arched his back and groaned.

He dropped back down into the creek and lay still.

"Crap," Nash said, and continued helping Samuel lead Zeb back toward their horses. "Maybe that wasn't the best decision, after all."

Chapter Nine

"YOU THINK HE'S gonna die, Nash?" Samuel asked, trotting his palomino a couple of feet off Nash's right stirrup.

The middle brother was staring fearfully at young Zeb, who rode double with Nash, who had his arms around the youngest Hollister brother so Zeb wouldn't tumble off onto the trail they were following back in the direction of the ranch headquarters. Zeb's horse, as well as the horses of the four dead hands, was trailing along behind Nash and Samuel, tied tail to tail.

Nash hadn't wanted to leave the horses in fear that Stillman's deputy would run one down and head on back to Clantick before Nash could get back after him. He'd been reluctant about going after the lawman and bringing big trouble down on the Triple H Connected, but now he had no choice.

If you're going to make an attempt on a law-man's life, it had better be a successful one or there'd be hell to pay. Besides, Nash was embarrassed. Him and six other men couldn't bring down one man, and they'd pretty much had him dead to rights. They must have underestimated him. Nash had heard that McMannigle had been an Indian fighter.

Well, he wouldn't underestimate him again.

Zeb had passed out from shock and pain, and he rode bobble-headed, chin with its little fringe of sandy-colored goatee dipped toward his chest.

"If he dies, Pa's gonna be madder'n he is already!"

"Samuel?"

"What?"

"Kindly shut up!" Nash shouted, leaning far out from his saddle and nearly getting up in his younger brother's face. He had too much to think about to listen to Samuel's anxious ramblings.

Samuel jerked back in his saddle with a start and stared at his older brother from beneath the brim of his Stetson. Too dumbfounded by the outburst to respond to it, he merely wagged his head once and then stared forward over his horse's twitching ears as they continued up the trail.

They gained the headquarters yard forty-five

minutes later, galloping the horses now, heading for the house. Despite the lateness of the hour, Nash saw shadows move in the lit windows of the long, log bunkhouse to his left, heard the door latch click then the hinges squawk as the door came open and several men stepped out onto the gallery, a couple holding rifles. The collie dog, Barney, came barking out from beneath the front porch of the house, the white spots on his coat glowing in the light from the windows bleeding into the otherwise dark yard.

Shadows moved in a few of the house's windows as well. The front door opened as Nash pulled his chestnut gelding to a halt in front of the veranda, Samuel moving along behind him, jerking the bridle reins of the first of the riderless horses he was trailing.

Much like the dog's white spots, Watt Hollister's gray hair glowed in the darkness as he stepped out onto the broad front porch, pulling the halved-log door closed behind him.

"You get him?"

Nash swung down from the saddle and caught his youngest brother as Zeb rolled toward him out of his saddle. With the unconscious Zeb stirring in his arms, groaning, Nash walked over and deposited his wounded youngest brother into Samuel's arms.

"Get him upstairs. Then send Carlton for Mrs. Wolfram."

Samuel nodded and carried his brother on up the veranda steps. The old man began cursing and when Samuel got Zeb inside, their mother began screaming shrilly. Ignoring the emotional outbursts, Nash turned to stare past Samuel toward the bunkhouse.

"Giuseppe over there?" he called as his mother's screams retreated deeper into the house.

The several men on the bunkhouse gallery shifted around, muttering. A shadow moved in the window nearest the bunkhouse's open door, and a short but thickset man tramped out onto the veranda, his long, black hair hanging to his broad, rounded shoulders straining the seams of his threadbare underwear shirt.

"How can I help, boss?"

Giuseppe Triejo's voice was deep, resonate, and thickly accented. The Mexican cowpuncher was the second lieutenant here at the Triple H Connected, behind the foreman, Blade Westin. Triejo had been many things in his long life on the frontier, including an army tracker—one of the best north of the Platte River--and while it wasn't openly discussed, everyone at the ranch knew he'd also been involved in several range wars down in Wyoming and Colorado.

That's why the xenophobic old man had hired him, why the former regulator was up here now, north of the Missouri River, working on a remote ranch and staying beyond the reach of both federal and territorial arrest warrants. The old man didn't mind hiring criminals as long as said criminal were discreet about their pasts and followed orders.

Giuseppe Triejo was getting old, pushing fifty. He preferred a quiet life these days, but he was still a hell of a tracker, arm wrestler, boxer—even against men half his age--and he was hell with his ancient, army-issue Spencer carbine. Nash had seen him at work against three rustlers they'd caught doctoring Triple H Connected brands down in the Missouri breaks earlier that summer. Three loud thumps from Triejo's old Spencer, and all three rustlers followed their spilled brains to the ground around their branding fire.

Nash said, "I need my best tracker on the trail of that Deputy Sheriff. We can't let him get back to town."

"A lawman, boss?"

"You got somethin' against killin' lawmen, Giuseppe?"

Nash could see only the short, broad-shouldered man's silhouette facing him, but he imagined a smile flicking across the old killer's craggy, pitted face with its mare's tail mustaches hanging beneath his chin. Giuseppe was known to harbor no soft feelings for any lawmen anywhere. His two younger brothers had been gunned down in cold blood by two deputy sheriffs in New Mexico, and a posse had tried to do the same to Giuseppe.

He'd outrun those he hadn't killed. He was still running.

"You want me to go tonight, boss?" the tracker asked in his deep, accented voice.

"If anyone can track him at night, it's you. The rest of us'll catch up to you sometime after sunrise. Take the Spearhead Trail to Cavalry Creek—that bend where you cut firewood last summer. He climbed that mountain to the south. He's on foot. I wanna make sure he stays that way until we've run him to ground. Just find him and pin him down till morning. Blaze, you go with him."

The stocky Mexican tracker turned, and his boots thudded, spurs chinging, as he headed back into the bunkhouse to gather his gear. Westin nodded his hatless head, flicked his cigarette into the yard where it bounced with a soft thump and sparked, and then he followed Giuseppe into the bunkhouse.

Nash turned and climbed the veranda steps. The lodge door opened, and Carlton Ramsay stepped out, donning his hat and wearing his deerskin overcoat. The middle-aged Carlton was the camp cook and housekeeper—an old cowboy too stoveup to punch cattle any longer. He was an old friend of Nash's father, one of the first men the old man had hired when he'd built up the Triple H Connected from little more than a one-room cabin and some breeding stock he'd driven up from Texas just before the war.

"That knee don't look good, Nash. Not one bit good. The boy needs me to fetch Doc Evans for him, not Mrs. Wolfram."

"No one goes to town till this is over. No word of this matter leaves the Triple H Connected."

"Nash, your little brother's gonna be a cripple without a good sawbones tendin' that knee."

"He'll likely be a cripple anyways, Carlton. Just fetch Mrs. Wolfram like I told you and quit crowin' about it."

"Well, your old man's crowin' about it." Ramsay raised his sheepskin collar to his hollow, gray-bristled cheeks against the night's chill and ambled toward the veranda steps. He smelled like whiskey, but then he usually smelled like whiskey this time of the night, as did Nash's father. Ramsay could still steer a buggy as far as the Wolfram place, two miles away. "He's crowin' about it plenty!"

Mikhail Wolfram punched cows most of the year for the Triple H Connected, and in return for his many years of service, Watt allowed him and his wife Maggie to have their own cabin and run a few chickens on Triple H Connected range. The old man valued loyalty above all else and did not hesitate to reward those most loyal to him.

As Carlton Ramsay dropped down the front steps, Nash could hear his father's bellows echoing throughout the house. Nash went inside to see old Watt coming down the stairs straight ahead and right, clinging to the rail as though it were the rail of a ship pitching in high seas. His liver-spotted face was livid. Spittle spewed from his walrus-mustached lips as he lifted each bony foot deliberately in turn.

". . . only daughter murdered—my dear, sweet Orleans butchered by a bluegum." He was wheezing, breathing hard. "I send my boys out on the simple chore of killin' one worthless coon with a badge—one damn deputy county sheriff who killed an innocent girl—and you bring your youngest brother home with a ruined knee! He'll never walk on that knee again if he lives the night, which is doubtful given how much blood he's lost!"

Nash said, "Go ahead and fall and break your neck, you old scudder," as he moved over to the large, black range and removed the coffee pot that remained all day until midnight on the warming rack—when it wasn't brewing a fresh batch.

The old man stopped and, sliding his lower jaw from side to side, glared from the foot of the stairs. "What did you say?"

"You heard me. Do us all a favor. Go on back up there and run down and snap your scrawny neck here on the kitchen floor!" Nash filled a large, white stone mug. He could hear his mother and Samuel talking in the upper story. Zeb was cursing like a gandy dancer on a hopping Friday night when all the half-breed doxies were going for half price.

Nash had to hand it to his youngest sibling— Zeb could curse with the best of them. He was a top hand, too. Good with a lariat as well as with a six-shooter, and out here you needed both.

But you had to know when to use the one and not the other. He thought the old man had gotten that wrong tonight. They should have merely threatened the deputy with a lynching, scared hell out of him. That would have been enough, under the circumstances. One of their own had died—the only girl in the family--so someone had to pay *something* or the Hollisters might begin to lose respect across the Hi-Line. But threat of a necktie party would have been enough.

A black man especially would have gotten a clear message he'd done something wrong.

No real laws would have been broken. At least, none that would warrant lawmen sniffing around out here. Now, all hell had broken loose. Now, who knew what was going to happen?

Now, they'd have to deal with Stillman.

The old man moved over to the stove and pulled a pothook from the wood box, raising it over his right shoulder and gritting his teeth, the pupils of both eyes as red as the fire in the range. "I oughta kill you for that, you ungrateful catamount!"

Nash glowered down at the old man, whose chin came up only to the eldest Hollister son's shoulder. "Put it down or I'll gut-shoot you, you old devil!"

"Nash, you stop talkin' to Pa that way!"

Nash looked up and behind the old man to see the curly-headed Samuel standing halfway down the stairs, glaring into the kitchen. His hat was off, his curly hair mussed and hanging in his eyes. "Stop it, you hear? We got enough trouble without you and Pa goin' at it like two bobcats in a cage!"

Nash grinned with menace at old Watt. The old man glanced over his shoulder at Samuel and then, his warty, liver-spotted, hawk-nosed face gaining a sheepish cast, slowly lowered the pothook and then dropped it back into the wood box.

Nash blew on his smoking mug as he went over and sat down at the long, oilcloth-covered table that seated the whole family and Carlton Ramsay and sometimes the foreman, Blaze Westin, as well. There was a wooden bowl of walnuts and a nutcracker on the table beside a hurricane lamp with a soot-stained, spruce green chimney.

Lost in his angry thoughts, Nash sipped his coffee and then cracked a walnut and ate it.

Meanwhile, Samuel came down, quickly removed his coat and then ladled water from the stove's warm water reservoir into a tin bowl. He set the bowl on the table and started opening and closing cabinet drawers. Old Watt poured himself a cup of coffee, splashed whiskey into it, returned the bottle to its shelf over the dry sink, and then walked into the open parlor where a small fire blazed in the stone hearth. He was muttering under his breath, talking to himself as he was doing more and more these days, Nash had noted.

As Samuel hurried up the stairs with the steaming bowl and several cloths wrapped over his forearm, the old man scowled at Nash from his worn, torn, bullhorn chair angled near the fire. "Your sister's dead! Doesn't that mean nothin' to you?"

His face was even redder than before.

"No, it don't mean crap to me."

"What?"

"I said it don't mean crap to me!" Nash said, breaking a walnut shell to smithereens that reined in tiny crumbs onto the oilcloth. "It don't mean crap to me because she's been dead a long time. Her soul, anyway. You killed her soul years ago, you dried up old peckerwood!"

Watt punched his chair arm with the edge of his fist. "How in the hell did I kill Orleans's soul?"

"By lockin' her up out here. By makin' sure she didn't go to town alone. Never alone. No boys from town or any of the ranchers could ever come out here and sit and talk to her for longer than fifteen, twenty minutes, and then either you or Ma had to be around to make sure nothin' improper happened!"

"That's how a girl is raised, Nash!"

"You didn't raise her, you old fool. You locked her up. Just like a cat from the hills, a girl—or a boy, for that matter—is going to go wild if you lock 'em up. And that's just what she did. I saw it happen just after Ma took that wooden spoon to her backside out in front of the bunkhouse when she caught her 'makin' eyes' at the half-breed, Dilloughboy, who you promptly run off the place. Couldn't you see she was gone for the boy?"

Nash gave a caustic laugh and obliterated another walnut. "And she was gone after that. Took off with him. Gone for good. Even helped him throw a gang together and start stealin' our beef! Hah!"

He shook his head and, chewing the walnut, blew on his coffee. "The girl had sand, I'll give her that. She's cut from the same cloth as me an' Zeb, only she's even tougher, more defiant. She wanted to ruin your withered up old ass and would have, too, if you didn't have so many pistoleros ridin' for you. Purely fittin'. Watt and Virginia Hollister's own well-brought-up daughter goes wild, throws in with a half-breed Injun from Canada, and tries to ruin her lovin' family!"

Old Watt punched his chair arm again. "Shut up. Shut you, d'you hear?"

"And you want to kill that deputy for killin' her when it's really you who killed her. You and Ma. Ah, hell, I reckon us brothers even had a hand in it. Only, this way it makes you feel better. Somebody actually killed her, and you can cover up your part in it—and defend her honor!—by goin' hog wild on the poor, badge-totin' sonofadevil who had no idea the bailiwick he was ridin' into when he rode out here with that coffin in his wagon. Gotta admit, I felt the same way when I first seen him. The black devil killed my sister.

I'm a Hollister, and he killed a Hollister, and by god, he should pay for that."

"He should, by god. He will, damnit, Nash!"

"Yes, he will, Pa. Oh, yes, he will! Hell, what choice do we have now? We done tried to kill him. If we don't finish him off, he'll report tonight's unseemly little events to his boss, Stillman, and then there'd be holy hell to pay. No, no. The fuse has done been lit. Now we gotta watch the whole keg explode and see where the Triple H Connected lands once the smoke clears."

"He killed your sister. He killed my sweet baby girl."

Nash looked at old Watt, who had turned now to the fire, his boots flat on the floor. He rested his arms and the hand holding his whiskey-laced coffee on the chair arms. He had a drawn, sadly pensive look on his ruined, ancient, dull-witted face.

Nash almost fell sorry for the old, half-demented codger. But then he remembered Orlean back when she was younger and her eyes had danced and she laughed at the drop of a hat. No more spirited filly had ever lifted dust at the Triple H Connected. Gradually as she matured, though. The fire had left the girl's eyes, and the flush of young womanhood and her innate zest for life was bleached from her cheeks by the invisible walls her parents and even her overly protective brothers had erected around her.

And then she was gone.

And now she was laid out dead in her old bed, in her old room, waiting to be planted on the hill behind the house where Nash's grandmother, Rose, had been buried along with the first Hollister child, stillborn.

"Don't worry, Pa," Nash said, holding his coffee in both hands and looking off at nothing, feeling as used up and dead as the girl upstairs. "He'll die. You'll get your revenge for your sweet baby girl. We'll feed his black carcass to the wolves. But I ain't doin' it for you. You keep that straight in your head."

He sipped the coffee again, licked his mustache. "I'm doin' it for the Triple H Connected."

Chapter Ten

McMannigle hobbled through the pines at the crest of the ridge.

The bullet in his upper right thigh felt like a hot blade being twisted and turned by some cunning torturer. Ignoring the wound for the moment, sucking sharp, pained breaths through gritted teeth, he dropped to his butt behind a tree and then, holding his carbine in both hands, twisted around to stare down the ridge in the direction from which he'd climbed.

Silence slid up the slope toward him.

There were only the quiets rasps of falling leaves and the faint wheezing of the breeze through the barren branches of the aspens. The glow from his fire was barely visible. It was merely a pinprick of pink light from this distance of a hundred yards or so and through the scattered conifers and deciduous trees stippling the incline.

He held his breath and pricked his ears sharply. Still, nothing. It didn't sound like anymore of the Triple H Connected men were moving toward him. They could be trying to get around him from each side, but Leon didn't think so. He'd likely killed the four climbing the slope for him. If he'd counted correctly before the shooting had started, that left only two upright. Two of the three Hollister brothers, most likely. He knew at least two of his ambushers had been Hollisters, so all three boys had likely been along to avenge their sister.

Since Leon had shot their brother, the other two were likely getting young Zeb back to the ranch headquarters.

"Sons of the devils."

McMannigle leaned his rifle against the tree and shifted his position until starlight shone on his wounded right thigh. The bloody wound glistened darkly halfway between his knee and his right front denims pocket. Most of that leg was numb. That foot felt heavy, and it was tingling painfully.

"Sons of the devils," Leon groused again.

Rage seared him to enflame the heat of the wound in his leg. They'd waited until he was a couple of miles from the ranch headquarters, and they'd bushwhacked him. Probably intended to kill him out here in this wild country a good twenty miles southwest of Clantick, where no one would find him.

Murderers.

Cold-blooded murderers.

But he was a fool to have banked on them not taking revenge for his killing the girl. Had he really thought he would have been able to square that with old Watt Hollister and his three sons?

Well, he had thought so. And he'd been three kinds of a fool to think it, too. Hadn't he been alive long enough to know the evil men were capable of?

He might have been a lawman, but that didn't mean much out here where most folks still took the law into their own hands. And then of course his being black had made the attempt on his life all the easier.

Leon groaned as he squeezed his thigh and watched the oily, dark, faintly glistening blood ooze up out of the hole. He'd taken a ricochet. He thought the bullet had ricocheted first off a rock and then off a tree bole. It was hard to tell, but he didn't think it had gone that deep into his flesh.

Groaning and grunting and cursing his fool-ishness at underestimating the savagery of the Hollisters, he tied his neckerchief around his thigh, just above the wound, to stem the blood flow. Then he slipped his bowie knife from his belt sheath and dug a box of stove matches from his shirt pocket where it was snugged down beside his hide makings sack.

He looked around once more to make sure he was alone up here, and then, hunkering down in the tree's thick shadow to be extra cautious, scraped the match to life on his thumbnail. He swiped the flame across the blade of his bowie knife several times until gray smoke curled up from the blade edge and he could smell the tang of hot steel.

"Okay, now," he said, raking breaths in and out of his lungs. "You ain't gonna pass out on me now, are ya, Leon? No, I'll say you ain't gonna pass out, because you done fought Apaches and you're no man to be trifled with. You pass out on me, Deputy, you'll just be provin' you got soft in these past five years since you moved north out of *Apacheria,* and you oughta just turn your badge in and hang up your shootin' iron and go live by yourself in one o' them empty shacks down by the river. Now, ain't that right, *Deputy?*"

He lowered the still smoking knife blade and heard himself mewl softly as he tried to widen the hole in his pantsleg. That wasn't happening, however. The area was too painful, and he'd only cause himself to pass out before he even started to dig for the bullet.

"Nah, nah, nah," he told himself. "Don't worry about the cloth. Just go in and probe for that bullet and pluck the damn thing outta there. You don't, you ain't goin' anywhere, and you'll just sit here on your ass and bleed dry. And then those sons of Hollister devils—pardon me, Miss Virginia, ma'am, since I know you're such a good Christian woman, an' all—will have accomplished exactly what they set out to do, which was to kill your black ass like you was no more than a calf-killin' coyote! *Ahhh, that hurts!*"

He tightened his jaws and stared down to watch his right hand plunge the tip of the knife directly into the wound. Mewling softly and breathing through his teeth, he shifted the knife handle this way and that and forced himself to hold his leg as still as stone.

That wasn't easy, given the searing pain that darted around as he shifted the knife, sending bayonets of hot agony up and down his leg and into his crotch and belly. He bit off his left glove and stuck his left index finger into the wound as well, and immediately felt the little chunk of lead just to the left of the hole. It was about an inch deep. Sighing and groaning deep in his throat, he worked his left finger as well as the knife until he'd rolled up the little chunk of lead that was causing him such a huge, wide world of grief onto the tip of the knife and held it there while he removed it.

"Well, I'll be a sonofabuck," Leon said, grinning, tears of misery rolling down his cheeks and beads of cold sweat popping out on his forehead. He held his bloody left thumb and index finger, between which he was holding the bloody, flattened bullet, up in front of his face. His hands was shaking as though from the ague.

"There you are you little devil! Why, I'll be a monkey's uncle. You ain't much bigger'n a black-eyed pea! Imagine somethin' so small grievin' me *so bad!*"

He tossed the bullet away, sucked another sharp breath, and then untied the neckerchief and moved it down over the wound, to stem the blood, and knotted it again.

"Oh, crap—I sure could do with a drink."

He looked around the tree and down the slope. He could no longer see the pink glow of his fire's coals. The fire had gone out. He had a bottle down there in his saddlebags. Did he dare retrieve it?

He raked a thumbnail down his bristly cheek, thinking it over. He doubted he'd make it back down to the camp and back up here on his bad leg. He'd best stay up here on high ground, from where he not only had the best view of the valley but a good place to hold off anymore riders.

He didn't doubt that old Hollister would send more men after him. Probably not till after sunrise, but since he couldn't move well, if any at all, the deputy had best stay right where he was. Maybe by morning he'd be feeling better and he could haul his wounded ass down the backside of the mountain and . . .

What?

Hide like a wounded bobcat?

How long could he stay alive out here, wounded and unable to get around, without food and water?

He looked down the slope again. He had both food and water down there. He also had a traveling flask of . . .

His eyes grew round. His lower jaw sagged.

He reached into his left coat pocket and, wrapping his hand around his hide-covered traveling flask, he shaped a delighted grin. He'd forgotten that earlier, just after he'd gathered firewood, he'd removed the flash from his saddlebags and slipped it into his coat pocket for easy access.

He pulled the flask out of the pocket, uncapped it, and took a long pull. Instantly, the fiery liquid spread a balm throughout his belly and tempered if only slightly the metronomic throb in his right leg. He sat back against the tree, took another pull, and then another. He shook the flask, judging the amount of remaining firewater, and then capped it and returned it to his coat pocket.

He settled farther back against the tree. Despite the cold night air and the pain in his leg, his eyelids grew heavy, as did his head. He drew a long, raspy breath, crossed his arms on his chest, dropped his chin, and felt sleep close over him like a dark, furry glove.

A voice woke him.

McMannigle opened his eyes and jerked his head up. It took him several seconds to get his bearings and to remember the cause of the heavy, throbbing agony in his right leg. A man's voice rose again behind him, and his heart thudded.

Someone was here.

He scrunched lower against the ground, gritting his teeth against the pain in his leg, and doffed his hat. He looked around the tree to stare down the slope toward the valley. He must have slept for over an hour, for the darkness was softening, the stars fading. Dark shapes shone against the faint gray bleeding into the valley from the east.

Leon shuttled his gaze slowly across the slope dropping away below him, pricking his ears, listening intently. Now he heard nothing except the rasp of the breeze picking up. Had he dreamt the voices?

A twig snapped dully.

McMannigle jerked his head hard left. A man-shaped shadow moved between two piñons, the gray light of the false dawn showing the fleece lining his heavy coat and flashing off the breech of the rifle in his hands. The man stopped, jerked his head up, lifted his rifle, shouting, "He's here!"

Boom!

The man's last word had been drowned by the thunder of McMannigle's rifle. The man's own rifle belched, stabbing flames toward the ground, blowing up dirt and pine needles three feet away from deputy. The man-made hiccupping sounds and his boots raked and thudded as he stumbled back through the pines on his spurs.

Leon sensed someone behind him now, moving toward him from the opposite side of the slope from the man he'd just shot. Using his Winchester as a crutch, he hoisted himself to his feet and, scrunching up his face against the pounding throb in his leg, feeling weak and sick to his stomach, he threw himself forward, dragging his wounded leg down the backside of the slope, pushing through pine branches.

Behind him, a rifle thundered. The slug screeched over his right shoulder and thumped loudly into an aspen bole. Leon scissored his left leg forward, dragging his right boot.

The rifle thundered again.

At the same time, McMannigle tripped over a deadfall, dropped hard, losing his rifle, and began rolling wildly down the bluff's steep back slope. The ground rapped him like a wildman with an axe handle. He had to suck the pain down deep to keep from screaming. Fortunately, he didn't roll far. He landed on a bench-like area, tumbled forward through several evergreen shrubs, and lay on his back, raking air in and out of his lungs like a landed fish.

Stifling a sob, he lifted his head.

His vision swam. Dirt and pine needles coated him. He looked down at his thigh. Blood oozed out around the neckerchief he'd tied over the wound. He looked around for his rifle but didn't see it. He lowered his right hand to his holster. Empty. He'd lost his Schofield revolver, too.

Crap . . .

Hay lay listening intently. There was no doubt that the second shooter was moving down the slope toward him. No doubt at all. Leon couldn't move, or he'd give away his position. All he could was lay here, wounded and bleeding and in silently screaming agony, and wait for the rifle-wielding killer to finish him.

Chapter Eleven

STILLMAN OPENED HIS EYES with a start.

He looked to the right, where a window shone with the gray-blue light of dawn.

"Good morning," said a female's warm, intimate, raspy voice above faint raking sounds.

Stillman blinked, squinted, blinked more sleep from his eyes. Fay's image clarified in the bedroom's heavy shadows. His tall, chocolate-haired, brown-eyed wife stood in front of an oval-shaped, wood-framed floor mirror just off the foot of their brass-framed bed, tilting her head and brushing her rich, flowing mane from the inside out.

She wore a flowered satin nightgown that only partly covered her burgeoning, pregnant form. Her belly containing their first child was as round as a large ball, and her bosom, large as nine-month old retriever pups, spilled over the top of the skimpy garment that Stillman had given her for their one-year anniversary. The right strap hung down her arm, and that side of the gown hung nearly all the way down the right breast as well.

Her bosom jostled as she tilted her head to the other side, and continued brushing, the rich lips of her long mouth quirking a warm smile as she blinked slowly.

"You should sleep some more."

Stillman pushed up to a half-sitting position, propped on his locked arms. He was fully dressed as he'd only lain down for a nap. He tore his gaze from the beautiful woman before him to the window. "How long I been out?"

"Only two hours. You came in after three. Two hours isn't enough sleep, Ben."

"Wasn't plannin' on sleepin' at all. It's Friday night, and I got two prisoners locked up in the calaboose."

"Leon's probably back, tending them."

"He's another thing I gotta check on. Gotta make sure that jasper's back."

Fay set the silver and tortoiseshell-backed brush on the dresser and walked over to the side of the bed. She did not pull the strap up her arm but let the nightgown dangle.

"He'll keep." She sat on the side of the bed and

leaned across her husband's belly to prop herself on her right arm. "You should sleep another hour, at least."

"I just came home for a cup of coffee and a bite to eat, you vamp. You led me up here, made me lay down, told me you'd wake me in an hour. You're a bad girl, Mrs. Stillman." He was caressing her voluptuous, infernally supple and erotic form with his eyes, and she delighted in it, showing all her fine, white teeth through a sparkling, sexy smile that lifted color in her high, perfectly sculpted cheeks.

"Guilty as charged. I just don't want you to wear yourself out. Soon, you're going to have a child to help me raise."

"His or her mother's likely gonna put me in a wheelchair."

"Oh, I think you can handle it." She leaned down and pressed her soft lips to his forehead. "Really, Ben—I think you should sleep. Leon's probably back from the Triple H Connected by now."

"Yeah, well, if he is, he's had a long night and needs his sleep worse than I do, though he don't deserve it—goin' against orders like he done."

Stillman pushed himself up a little farther and started to roll toward the edge of the bed. Faith placed her hand on his chest, pushing him back down.

"Hold on. If you can't sleep, we can try something else to help you relax, mon cherie. Relax and invigorate you, oui?" Faith, nearly twenty years younger than Stillman, hailed from a wealthy French ranching family down around the Powder River country, and her earthy, ranch-born-and-bred femininity coupled with her seductive French blood was never more apparent than in the main bedroom of the Stillman house. The bed of which Stillman was sure they'd bust into a pile of jackstraws before they got their second bun in the oven.

Lowering his hand to caress her large, hard belly, feeling a warmth rising in his loins, he said, "Might not be such a good idea . . . for a woman in your condition, I mean." He looked at her, arching one brow, desire at work in him. "You think?"

Faith blinked once again, slowly, and leaned down to press her lips to his. She prodded his teeth with her tongue and nibbled his mustache as she pulled her head away. She smoothed his thick, gray-brown hair back from his temples, kissed his forehead, and then slid the left strap of her nightgown all the way down her arm.

"Yes, but you know as well as I do, *mon cherie,* that there are other things we can do." She ran her tongue across her upper lip and then began unbuckling his belt. "I believe we've gotten quite good at it, in fact, no?"

Stillman lay his head back on the pillow and groaned.

～～～

A half hour later, Stillman clicked his Colt's hammer back.

"All right, come on out of there before I start loosin' lead. Come on—I see you back there!"

Stillman was sitting his horse at the corner of Gaylord Street and Clantick's main drag, First Street, and he was aiming his revolver across the front of a barbershop on his right, toward the ends of a muffler he could see blowing out of an alley mouth. He'd just ridden down from his and Faith's little ranch on a bluff north of Clantick when, approaching First Street, he'd glimpsed the shadowy figure dart into the alley between the barber shop and a little tobacco shop just beyond it.

The blowing muffler ends disappeared, as though whoever was standing in the alley had stepped back farther away from the mouth still gauzy with early morning shadows.

"I'm not going to tell you again!" Stillman warned. "Come on out of there now!"

Haltingly, a clay-clad figure emerged from the mouth of the alley. The slender person wore a white knit cloth cap, the muffler, and a long, gray coat. Long, sandy-blond hair blew around the girl's head in the wind. Sheepishly, she lifted her dimpled chin, and smiled a little too brightly, slapping a hand to her chest. "Oh, Ben—it's you!"

The sun just now rising behind Stillman shone in her pale blue eyes.

"Evelyn?"

"I didn't know it was you. Didn't even recognize your voice with all the trash blowin' in the alley."

Stillman depressed his gun hammer and returned the Colt to its holster. "What're you doin' out here so early, actin' so . . . secretive? You ain't plannin' a holdup, are ya?" He chuckled.

"Oh, no—nothin' like that, Ben." Evelyn looked around, her cheeks flushed with embarrassment, and she appeared to be straining for an explanation before she hooked a nervous thumb over her shoulder and said, "I was . . . I was just comin' from the doc's place."

"The doc's place?"

"Yeah . . . I . . . uh . . . brought him breakfast. You know how he likes Sam's venison liver and onions. We had some leftover, so I took 'em up to him."

Stillman canted his head in disbelief. "You tellin' me, little lady, that Doc Evans is up at this hour?" The sawbones was a notorious drunk who, between patients, was known to either frequent the Clantick doxiehouses till late at night or mid-morning of the next day, or to stay home and read the books in his vast classical library and drink brandy till he passed out.

"Yeah, well . . . he was awake, all right." Evelyn smiled, the flush in her cheeks deepening. "I was a little surprised by that myself. Thought I'd have to leave the vittles on his table. Oh, well—I reckon I'd best be heading back to the café now, Ben. I wasn't sure who you were, and it was such a wild Friday night, I thought you might be one of them wild track layers."

She'd stepped out onto the street and was now making her way past the sheriff straddling the big bay. She headed in the direction of Sam Wa's café. "No girl is safe with them in town!"

"No, I reckon not," Stillman said, scowling after her. He'd be damned if she didn't seem odd. He'd seen Evelyn and Evans together quite a bit, usually just having coffee together in the café.

They wouldn't have struck up a dalliance, would they?

Stillman wiped the thought from his mind. Everyone knew that the doc had promised his frequent medical partner, the Widow Kemmett, that they'd be married soon. Not even Evans, whose morals were unquestioned only because everyone pretty much knew he didn't have any, would do something that lowdown, scoundrel, dirty, and cruel—breaking Katherine Kemmett's heart in favor of a much younger girl.

Of course, Stillman didn't have much room to judge a man harshly for choosing a younger woman though he'd always felt that he hadn't chosen Faith so much as Fate had chosen her for him.

And, of course, he hadn't promised himself to another woman . . .

Ruminating, he clucked Sweets ahead and headed south toward the jailhouse, hoping he'd either find his deputy there or some sign that he'd made it back to town in one piece. As Stillman pulled up to the hitchrack fronting his office, he saw a horse standing in front of Auld's Livery & Feed Barn on the opposite side of the street and a half a block farther west.

The sun had risen enough that the sheriff could see that the horse was a beefy skewbald. It had probably gotten out of Auld's paddock during the night, took a little run around town, and had now returned for breakfast. Auld or his sometimes assistant, Olaf Weisinger, would likely let the horse in when the livery opened for business at eight.

Stillman tied Sweets to the hitchrack, unlocked the office door, and headed on inside to find no sign that McMannigle had returned to town. If he had, he'd surely have built up the fire in the stove that stood in the middle of the rear cellblock, which was housing the two troublemakers from Sam Wa's Café—Seymore Scudder and the barrel-shaped, freckle-faced gent, Llewelyn Sweney. Both hardcases were market hunters, though they'd be out of a job at least until the circuit judge pulled through Clantick and tried them, which likely wouldn't be for another week or so.

"How good of you to put in an appearance, Sheriff," griped Scudder from behind the cross-shaped bandage that Doc Evans had placed over his nose and cheekbones and up around his swollen, bloodshot eyes. "If you'd shown up a few minutes late, we'd likely be frozen up stiff as corpses!"

Stillman had just pulled his hand away from the stove, which he'd banked early this morning before he'd gone home and was still warm, though far from hot. It was a little chilly in the cellblock, but his two prisoners had been in no danger of freezing to death.

Sweney sat on the edge of his cot in the cell beside Scudder's, two army blankets draped over his thick shoulders. His right arm, which Stillman had drilled with a .44 round, was in a sling. "We got rights, Sheriff. The right not to freeze to death while we're incarcerated in this rat-infested shack you call a jailhouse!"

"And we'd like coffee and some pancakes and eggs and a big slice of ham!" added Scudder.

"You two got a little uncomfortable this mornin', did you?" Chunking split pine logs through the potbelly stove's open door, Stillman chuckled. "Well, I'm real sorry about that. To think that I'd go and let the fire burn down on two such honorable, upstanding citizens locked up in my jailhouse. That burns me with shame, purely it does."

He chuckled again as he used one of the logs to stir the coals inside the stove.

"Go to hell, Stillman," bellowed Sweney. "My arm hurts somethin' fierce, and it hurts worse when I'm cold and hungry!"

When Stillman had the stove fire burning and the iron stove ticking, he closed the door. "No, Sweney." He grinned without mirth as he stared through strap iron bands of the cell door at the square-headed, pugnacious, freckle-faced gent. "You'll get fed when I feel like feedin' ya."

Stillman walked back through the cellblock and into his office, closing the stout, wooden door on the prisoners' chorus of bellowing curses, and turned the key in the lock.

He was paying no attention to the hardcases' complaints. His mind was on Leon. It wasn't all that odd that his deputy hadn't yet made it back to town, as it had been a dark night and the Triple H Connected was a good twenty-mile ride southwest, over and around some fairly high Two-Bear Mountain ridges. Likely, Leon would have stopped and camped for the night and started back toward town at dawn.

Stillman would likely see him soon. And when he did, he'd give him one hell of a tongue lashing for disobeying orders, though deep down Stillman understood why he'd done what he'd done. But orders were orders. McMannigle would be expecting the reprimand.

Still, the sheriff felt more than a twinge of uneasiness in his belly.

Instead of building a fire in the main office, he walked out onto the front stoop, looking around at the street over which the sun was sliding purple shadows into alley mouths and up against building fronts. Smoke from breakfast fires wafted in the breeze, rife with the tang of pine and cedar cut in the creek bottoms and mountains. Several shopkeepers were sweeping their porches or arranging merchandise into outdoor displays.

Reaching inside his coat for his makings sack, Stillman glanced along the street to his right. He left the pouch in his pocket. The burly, bearded, overall-clad Emil Auld was standing just outside his open barn doors, appraising the skewbald facing him. Auld had a hand on a rope attached to the horse's hackamore, and he was sort of leaning back and looking down, inspecting the horse's hooves.

"Auld!"

Stillman dropped down into the street and started walking toward the barn, gradually increasing his pace as his heart quickened. As he approached the liveryman, who was raking his faintly perplexed gaze between Stillman and the horse, Auld said, "Deputy McMannigle—he's back?"

"No, he's not back," Stillman said.

"This here is the horse I gave him to pull his wagon."

Stillman stopped in his tracks. "No wagon?"

Auld looked around, pursing his lips and shrugging. "Do you see a wagon?"

"Dammit!"

Stillman swung around and jogged back to the jail office. He went inside and quickly stuffed some trail supplies and two boxes of .44 shells—one for his revolver, one for his Henry rifle—into a pair of saddlebags, and grabbed his bedroll hanging from a coat hook by a leather thong. Heading back outside, he closed and locked the door behind him, slung the saddlebags behind his cantle, tied the bedroll over them, and stepped into the leather.

He stopped with the horse half-turned away from his office, scratching his chin and scowling.

He needed a deputy . . .

He neck-reined the big bay toward Sam Wa's Café, and spurred the horse into a gallop, hooves drumming in the still-quiet but brightening street, riding through tufts of tangy chimney smoke. At Sam Wa's, he checked the horse down, swung out of the saddle, mounted Sam's little, sun-silvered boardwalk and pushed the door open, causing the cowbell to clatter.

Evelyn was just then pouring coffee for her only two customers at a table along the wall to the right and about halfway down the room.

"Evelyn?"

The young blond, her hair pinned up, turned to Stillman. Again, her face acquired a flushed, sheepish look, causing the sheriff to half-consciously speculate about what had happened over at the doc's place. "Ben?" Smoke curled from the spout of the big, black coffee pot she held by a potholder in her right hand.

"Consider yourself deputized."

"Huh?"

The extroverted, eminently affable and big-hearted girl was well liked throughout the town if not the county. Evelyn was like a receptive bar tender in that she knew most everyone's secrets and troubles, did not flinch at doling out advice based on lessons she'd learned from her own troubled past, and her forthright manner commanded moral authority. Stillman knew that if he could trust anyone to keep the peace when both he and Leon were away, that person was Evelyn Vincent.

"I have to head out to the Two-Bears--"

"Is it Leon?" Evelyn asked, eyes wide with concern.

"Yeah, it's Leon. Anyone causes a ruckus between now and when I get back, beetle your brows at 'em. If that doesn't work, use that bung starter you keep behind the counter. If *that* doesn't work, send Sam and his meat cleaver. Good luck. Be back soon!"

He pinched his hat brim to the girl staring at him with her mouth agape and went out and closed the door. He mounted Sweets and spurred the horse west at a full gallop, causing a couple of dogs to run after him, nipping at the bay's hocks and barking.

Chapter Twelve

On his back on the side of the mountain, Leon waited.

He seemed to be waiting a long time, his back against the cold ground, blood oozing from the wound in his leg, before he heard the faintest foot tread—the very slight crunch of gravel and pine needles crackling softly under a man's stealthy step. The deputy had begun to wonder if the second stalker—were there only two or were there more closing around him?—was coming for him, or was he may be waiting atop the ridge for him to show himself so he could shoot him from long distance with the rifle?

He was here. Only a few feet away.

There was another footfall so faint that if it hadn't been so early-morning quiet and the birds had not started chirping yet, the deputy wouldn't have heard it.

Having neither his revolver nor his rifle, he'd slid his bowie knife from his belt sheath. He squeezed it in his right hand up around that ear, the blade pointed straight above his head.

His heart thudded slowly, heavily.

Suddenly, the barrel of a rifle was thrust through the trees screening Leon. The rifle roared, lapping flames. The slugs screeched over Leon and chewed into the trees and spanged off rocks beyond him. Leon lay flat, gritting his teeth and squeezing his eyes closed, waiting for the man to lower his rifle's barrel.

When he did that, that would be the end.

Leon's heart raced. His hand sweated around the handle of the bowie knife.

As suddenly as it had started, the rifle's rat-aplan ceased after six shots. McMannigle had been counting the rounds the way a man sealed alive in a coffin counts the nails being hammered through the lid.

The din hadn't died for much over a second before the deputy lifted his head and, with a grunt, flicked the bowie knife two-fingered from beside his right ear. The knife whistled as it tumbled through the air, crunching through the thin screen of branches in front of him.

There was a crunching thud.

A sucked breath. A gasp.

There was a clattering thump as the man dropped his rifle. He stumbled forward through the screen, the piñon branches parting like a tattered curtain. The man was short and thick, with heavy, round shoulders and long, greasy black hair dangling from beneath his black slouch hat with a beaded leather band around the crown. The man's face was massive and hideously ugly, with wide-set eyes, a wedge-shaped nose, and many deep pockmarks in his red-dark skin.

He staggered into the slight clearing in which Leon lay, staring wide-eyed up at the man, who wore a dark wool, three-point capote that hung to his knees. The wooden handle of McMannigle's knife stuck out of the man's upper left chest. Leon thought he'd missed the man's heart, but frothy blood was bubbling up around the blade, soaking the man's coat. The stuff that didn't soak into the wool dribbled down the front.

The man stared down at Leon blankly at first, but then his oily black eyes flashed, and his mustached mouth curled a wry grin. He lifted his right hand, wrapped it around the knife handle, and made a strained expression, narrowing his eyes, as he tugged at the bowie. Pulling on the handle, he gritted his teeth. His hand quivered as he gave a yelp and, with great effort, pulled the blade out of his chest with a wet sucking sound.

Tears welled in his dark eyes, dribbled down his cheeks.

Blood dripped thickly from the bowie's wide blade.

The stocky Mexican glared down at McMannigle, took another shambling step toward him, and started to lift the knife threateningly. Before he could get it half-raised, he dropped with another yelp to his knees and blinked his eyes as he continued to glare down at Leon, gritting his teeth.

The Mexican's torso sagged forward. McMannigle rolled onto his left shoulder a half-second before the big Mexican shooter landed with a heavy thud and a sigh onto the ground Leon had just vacated.

The Mexican's broad, rounded shoulders wobbled. His legs shook, he made a gurgling sound, and lay still.

Leon rolled onto his belly, got his knees under him, and heaved himself up until he was half-standing, extending his wounded right leg out to the side, keeping as much weight off it as he could. He tightened the bandage over the wound, breathing hard, groaning, and then looked around, listening. He couldn't hear much above his own heavy, raking breaths, but he thought he must be alone.

If there were others out here, they would have shone themselves by now.

He stared down at the inert Mexican. The sun was nearly up now, and its soft, blue-gray light showed the blood pooling on the gravel and pine needles beneath the dead Mex's chest and belly. Leon groaned again as he picked up his bowie knife, cleaned it on the dead man's coat, and slipped it back into his belt sheath.

He pulled the man's Smith & Wesson and stuffed it into his own holster. His heart beat insistently now, hopeful. These two must have horses tethered somewhere at the foot of the mountain. McMannigle had to get to a mount and get started back to Clantick before he bled dry.

"Easier said than done, hoss," he told himself.

He pushed through the screen of branches and stumbled over the dead Mexican's rifle. Leon picked up the Winchester Yellowboy, made sure there wasn't a shell in the chamber, and then used the rifle as a crutch as he got started back up the steep side of the bluff.

The severe incline winded him quickly. His head pounded and the slope rose and fell around him. He was dizzy from blood loss, but he pushed on, maneuvering sideways up the slope, using the rifle barrel to hoist himself and then sliding the wounded left leg up behind him. It was excruciatingly slow and painful going and he had to stop several times to rest and let the hammering in his skull subside.

He finally made it, and after a two-minute breather, leaning on the rifle, he started down the front side of the bluff, which was far less steep than most of the backside. He leaned hard on the rifle with every step, but he made fast progress, noting with a scowling disdain a couple of the men he'd killed last night. By the time he reached the bottom of the bluff, the sun was up and warming the frosty air, gilding the leaves slowly tumbling from the aspens lining the sparkling creek. The sky was faultless, cerulean blue.

It would have been a damned fine morning if he wasn't losing blood and strength fast, he vaguely opined as he looked around for his now-dead stalkers' horses.

He shuffled upstream from a man who lay dead in the shallow water, dropped down beside the creek, and, though it aggravated the pulsating burn in his thigh, he lowered his head to the water and drank thirstily. The water so cold he thought his teeth would crack, but he drank his fill, feeling nourished and ever-so-slightly invigorated.

He looked at the dead man whose limbs bobbled in the current. His faded red neckerchief snaked six inches out in the current. The man's eyes were half-open, and his mouth was slack beneath his sandy-brown mustache, giving him a sad, longing look.

"Damn, that's good," Leon jeered, smacking his lips as water dribbled down the corners of his mouth. "A drink of fresh spring water on a purty mountain morning. That's a pleasure you'll never have again, my friend. Should have left this darkie well enough alone!"

McMannigle gave a disdainful chuff then limped across the creek, paused beside the cold, gray remains of his fire, and reached into his saddlebags for several strips of deer jerky. He ate one whole strip standing over the bags and washed it down with several swigs of whiskey from his flask. Then, chewing another strip, he shuffled out away from the fire ring and into the clearing, chewing and grunting and dragging his right boot across the short grass and gravel, weaving between bristly pine shrubs.

He found the horses tied near the trail to a single blowdown pine out of sight from the clearing.

"Oh," Leon said, tears of joy veiling his eyes and running down his cheeks.

He didn't know when last he'd been so happy to see a saddle horse. And here were two—a

handsome roan and a short, broad-barreled
Appaloosa, which had probably belonged to the
stocky Mexican. Their breeze-brushed coats
shimmered in the golden light of the rising sun.

Both horses had been standing facing the
blowdown pine, but now they were staring at the
black man shambling toward them, leaning on a
rifle and dragging his right leg around which the
green neckerchief was tied. They stared darkly,
twitching their ears. Suddenly, the roan lifted its
head and whickered.

"Easy, fellas," Leon said. "Easy, now, easy."

He looked at the reins tied to separate branches of the blowdown. Neither set appeared to be
tied all that tightly. The horses were likely well
trained, and the tying of the reins had only been
a precaution.

Frightened by the stranger shuffling toward
him, the roan whinnied and pulled at the reins,
which held but the deputy could see the slipknot
loosen a little.

Oh, no.

"Hold on, now," Leon pleaded, panting, keeping his voice down as he slowed his pace. "Hold
on. Easy. I'm just gonna take these reins here . . .
slip them over the branch . . . like *that!*"

Relief washed over him when he'd grabbed the
roan's reins, slick from a fresh greasing. But then

the roan jerked its head up sharply and lunged back away from the pine. Leon managed to hold onto the reins, but the roan's lunge pulled him sharply forward. He lost his footing, wounded leg barking madly, and fell in a heap. Fire shot up and down his leg. Somehow, he'd managed to hold onto the slick reins, and, dropping the rifle, he closed both his hands around them, wrapping them around his knuckles.

He wouldn't give up the reins if the horse pulled both his arms out of their sockets!

"Oh, now, don't do that, hoss!" Leon ground his teeth together. "Don . . . don't do that, now, you scoun . . . I mean, you fine-lookin', precious animal!"

He let the horse's pressure on the reins help pull him to his feet. He stood still for a time, holding the reins but neither saying nor doing anything, just letting the horse relax with him present. When the beast had grown relatively calm, Leon limped slowly over to the left stirrup. The horse whickered and backed away. The deputy froze again, stress tightening all the muscles in his back and filling him with dread.

If he could not get himself mounted, he was a goner.

More riders from the Triple H Connected would likely be heading this way soon. He had to get back to town, inform Ben what had happened and then get himself over to Doc Evans's place for tending.

If it had been his left leg that had been wounded, he doubted he would have been able to get mounted, especially with the horse curveting as though to rid himself of the stranger who smelled like fresh blood, but Leon managed to toe the left stirrup and, with a shrill sigh he swung his wounded right leg over the horse's rump and got the toe of that boot in its corresponding stirrup.

He whistled raspily, neck-reined the jittery horse around, and pulled it out onto the wagon trail, directing it northeast, in the direction of town. The horse broke into a trot, ears and tail up, muscles bunching tensely beneath the saddle.

The horse's jouncing felt like a twisting knife in the wound, so he slowed the horse to a walk, and took another couple of pulls from his flask, draining it. He tossed it away with a wince of regret. It would take longer, walking instead of trotting, but at least he'd arrive in town with a pint or two of blood left in his veins.

Fatigue lay heavy on the deputy's shoulders. Before he realized what was happening, his eyes were closing and he was leaning forward to snug his cheek down taut against the roan's mane, letting his arms dangle both sides of the pole.

He became aware that the horse was no longer moving.

Leon jerked his head up.

The sun was high and warm.

He looked around, blinking his eyes. A sledge-hammer of shock smashed into his forehead, and his belly filled with the hot tar of dread when he realized that the horse had not taken him back to town but right into the Triple H Connected compound!

The horse stood near one of several corrals, nose to nose with a horse inside the corral. Smoke issued from the main house's broad stone hearth only fifty, sixty yards away. A chaise with its top down stood near the front porch, a black horse in its traces.

Anxiety ripped through the deputy. He looked around for his horse's reins. They were on the ground, cracked and broken. The horse had apparently dragged them and stepped on them.

"Oh, crap," Leon said, glancing at the house once more. He thought he saw a curtain move in an upper story window. Someone had seen him.

His head swam. His heart pounded. He had to get the reins.

He swung awkwardly, painfully down from the saddle, looking around for the gallblasted dog he'd seen before when he'd come with the dead girl in the wagon, and who'd barked at him no end. As he reached for the reins, everything went black and silent. He was only vaguely aware of his knees, and then his head hitting the ground.

And then he was out like a blown lamp, sound asleep in the middle of the Triple H. Connected headquarters.

Chapter Thirteen

NASH HOLLISTER HELD up his right hand and drew back on his horse's reins with the left one.

As his gelding slowed to a walk, the dozen or so riders—every man who'd been left in the Triple H Connected bunkhouse—slowed their own horses behind him. Nash studied the Appaloosa tethered to the blowdown pine ten yards off the side of the trail.

The Appy belonged to Giuseppe Triejo. Nash glanced around for Blaze Westin's mount, saw nothing but breeze-jostled grass and shrubs and pine-clad slopes rising around him. The eldest Hollister son had no idea why both men wouldn't have either been mounted or on foot, but he'd likely find out soon enough.

He touched spurs to his zebra dun's flanks and galloped around the base of the pine-stippled ridge and into the clearing, seeing the deputy's wagon on the right, about fifty feet from the fire ring and strewn gear. The stream chuckled over rocks beyond the fire and the gear. Blood stained the ground to the right of the fire, at the base of the southwestern slope.

His brother Zeb's blood. Blood from his youngest brother's ruined knee. Nash vaguely wondered if the kid was still alive. If he lived, he'd be a cripple for the rest of his life. Nash wasn't sure the kid wouldn't be better off dead.

"Head on up the ridge," he ordered the men around him, their breath as well as their horses' breath pluming in the chill, sunny air, aspen leaves tumbling around them to scrape along the rocks lining the streambed. "Spread out. That's where Westin and Triejo would have gone lookin' for a sign. They likely marked where they picked up the deputy's trail with a neckerchief tied to a branch, so keep your eyes open."

The men spurred their horses on around the cold campfire and across the stream, water droplets sparkling like diamonds. They glanced down at where Morgan still lay on the rocks in the creek, arms and legs spread and being nudged by the current. He stared sadly up at the blue sky arching over him.

Hooves clattered over rocks and then the men's horses grunted and snorted as they lunged on up the ridge, weaving amongst the piñons, aspens, firs and occasional boulders. They rode abreast, spread out away from each other, looking around for that trail marker. A couple of men gestured to the other three dead Triple H Connected men, conversing amongst themselves.

Nash remained mounted near the fire ring mounded with gray ashes. There was no point in him climbing the ridge. That's why he had men working for him. There was little doubt in his mind that the grisly little opera that had played out here had come to an end earlier this morning. The deputy was likely dead and Triejo and Westin were probably riding back in this direction with the black man's body draped over one of their horses.

Nash's only reason for riding out here was to make sure that all the loose ends were tied. He had to make sure the deputy did not get back to Clantick. If that happened—well, Nash didn't even want to think about what would happen, then. It couldn't happen, that's all.

What a damn mess.

And he'd been a part of it.

He should have stopped it before it had even begun, refusing the old man's orders to hunt the deputy down. But Nash had been drunk on the same emotion old Watt had been drunk on, learning that the Negro deputy had killed Orleans.

A black man killing Nash's sister, his family's pride and joy . . .

It had been a misdirected fury, but fury just the same. Now, he was filled with a vague but noxious sense of dread and menace. It had a tight hold on him, and it had put him in one hell of a bad mood. He didn't wonder consciously about what this all would lead to, but somewhere deep in the bowels of his consciousness, he was working on it, all right. The unoiled gears were grinding away, squawking and clattering.

He hadn't slept a week since the botched ambush.

Now, hearing his men calling back and forth to each other as they climbed the slope on the far side of the stream, Nash hooked his right leg over his saddlehorn, hauled out his makings sack, and built a cigarette while he brooded. He scratched a match to life on the wooden head of his saddlehorn frame, which was protruding through a torn seam in the leather—winter was the time for such chores as tack repair--and touched the match to the end of his quirley.

"Boss!"

Blowing smoke into the cool air, Nash lifted his gaze to the ridge. He could see only one man

sitting his white-socked black horse at the top of
the bluff, waving to him broadly with one arm.

Nash lowered his right boot to its stirrup,
and, casually puffing the quirley, touched spurs
to his dun. He rode across the stream, not glancing at Morgan still wallowing there, and began
climbing the ridge, letting the horse pick its own
course through the trees and brush snags. When
he'd gained the ridge crest, he saw several men
sitting their horses just down the bluff's steep
backside.

They all looked grim; none seemed eager to
make eye contact with him.

"You find Triejo's trail?"

"Nah, boss," said Luther Simonson, the man
who'd waved. "We found Triejo."

"Westin's over here," said a man standing atop
the ridge beyond Simonson, flanked by a clump
of tall fir trees and shaggy piñons. He glanced
over his left shoulder to indicate something in
the trees behind him and stretched a bitter grin.
"Bullet in the neck."

A cold anvil dropped in Nash's belly. The hair
along the back of his neck pricked.

He looked down the slope where three men
were standing in a ragged circle, holding their
horses' reins and gazing grimly up the steep slope
toward Nash. Rather than ride his own horse

down the steep declivity, the elder Hollister son swung heavily, dreadfully down from his saddle, dropped his reins, and tramped down the slope. He almost fell on a patch of slippery grass, almost swallowed the quirley in his teeth, and cursed as he threw out his arms to catch himself.

The three men sat their horses outside another patch of scraggly cedars and piñons. Two backed their horses away from each other in the bowl-shaped depression, making way for Nash. He pushed through the branches, nervously puffing the quirley clamped between his jaws, and felt that anvil in his belly flop onto its side when he stared down at the broad back and the back of the head of Giuseppe Triejo.

Nash clenched his fists at his sides.

He turned and walked back out of the trees and shrubs and looked around. His heart was hammering. "Anyone seen Triejo's horse?"

All the men around him looked around.

"No," one of them said dully.

Nash started climbing the slope toward his dun.

"What about the lawman?" asked one of the mounted men behind Nash.

"He's headed for town," Nash bit out, nostrils swelling, anxiety causing his heart to beat faster. "On the Mex's horse." He threw his arm violently forward. "Come on, damnit! We gotta find him before he gets to town!"

⌒～⌒

"Gotta get you up, Deputy. Hey, can you hear me? Gotta get you up or you'll be dead right quick!"

Leon had heard the high, Southern-accented, female voice as though she were calling softly to him from the top of a deep well that he lay at the bottom of. He had to be dreaming, but when someone began tugging on his arm, rolling him onto his side, he opened his eyes.

Nothing but a lemon-gray blur. But then the face of a pretty young woman—brown-haired, hazel-eyed, snub-nosed—clarified before him. She wore a man's tan felt hat and tight braids draped down her chest, over an open, buckskin jacket showing a vest and a man's hickory shirt. She wore gray knit gloves with one torn finger, women's scuffed brown half boots, and a gray skirt.

She was tugging on his arms with both hands, glancing over and beyond him. "If you don't want to die out here, you'd best do as I say! Ole Barney's bound to come back from one of his rabbit-huntin' trips and kick up a ruckus!"

McMannigle sat up and looked in the direction she was looking. The Hollister cabin sat large and formidable at the other end of the yard. A buggy with its top down sat in front of the porch. He just then remembered where he was, and as he began trying to heave himself to his feet, the girl crouched under his left arm and, grunting, helped him up and over to the side of a log shed that was likely a blacksmith shop or tack shed.

Here, he was out of sight of both the bunkhouse and the yard.

He leaned back against the shed and then fatigue caused him to sag down onto the lumber that had been piled there and around which brome grass and lamb's ear had grown tall. The girl ran back and, canting her pretty, hazel eyes toward the house again, grabbed the reins of Leon's appropriated horse and led the mount, clucking, out of the main yard and over toward Leon.

Clamping a hand over his wound, gritting his teeth, he looked up at the girl whom he judged to be not much over twenty. "Who're . . . you . . . and . . . why . . .?"

"Hush!"

Holding the horse's reins, she began pulling on his arm again. He heaved himself to his feet, the ground and the horse pitching around him, the roan whickering anxiously.

"Can you get back up there?" the girl asked,

glancing at the saddle.

McMannigle said half-heartedly that he thought he could. She turned the horse around so that it's left side faced him and the horse itself was facing back toward the yard. The deputy stepped up onto the lumber pile, and from there to the stirrup, and from the stirrup—with an agonized groan—onto the saddle.

"Hold on, now," the girl admonished him, and, leading the horse by its reins, turned it around.

Leon grabbed the saddlehorn as the girl led him and the horse off behind the shed, away from the yard and the corrals. The deputy's head hung heavily, and he realized that he was lapsing in and out of semi-consciousness, only vaguely aware that he and the horse were being led down a hill through sometimes-thick brush. They crossed what must have been a coulee or a creek bed at the bottom of the hill—he could hear and smell running water, mud, and the musk of verdant growth—and then she admonished him to hold on again, and he was pushed back in the saddle as they climbed a steep slope.

He hunkered low over the horse's mane.

He must have lapsed even deeper into semi-unconsciousness, for, while he sporadically heard and saw things and smelled things around him— the chirping of birds, the passing of evergreen trees, the sweet fetor of some dead, rotting animal maybe lying in the brush near the trail the girl was leading him down—time slipped away from him. He was half-aware of being helped down off the horse, and then he heard the clomping of his own dragging boots and raking spurs on what must have been a wooden floor. He smelled pent up air and wood mold and then the sweaty stench of old wool.

For a time, he was aware of nothing except the pain in his leg. It was as though the world had died around him, leaving only his throbbing wound and a nebulous dream of running from Apaches while trying to pull an arrow from his leg, and they were getting closer and closer, whooping and hollering . . .

Suddenly, his right leg started burning.

He gave a loud, shrieking grunt, and lifted his head and opened his eyes to see the girl sitting beside him.

"Hold still! Hold still!"

Placing her bare hand on his chest, she pushed him back down onto the cot he was on. She'd cut his pants open, revealing the bloody wound, and now she was dabbing at it with a cloth.

Each time she dabbed, Leon felt as though a fire burning under his heart were being fanned. He sucked air through his teeth and stared at the herringbone pattern ceiling adorned with cobwebs in which old flies, dirt, soot, and even ancient brown leaves and a piece of yellowed newspaper hung suspended.

"Where am I?" he asked as the girl worked on his leg.

"This is Watt Hollister's original homestead cabin. He and Carlton Ramsay built it after Watt ran his first herd of cattle up from Texas."

Leon clenched the wool blanket beneath him in his fists as the girl continued to clean the wound. "Who're you?" he asked.

"I'm Nash's wife." She looked up at him and smiled as she wrung the bloody cloth out in the tin basin resting on a chair beside the cot. There was an open whiskey bottle there as well.

"I'm Carrie Anne Hollister," she said, and winked. "Pleased to make your acquaintance, Deputy." She frowned then, queerly, dramatically. "Though I'm sure the pleasure is all mine."

Chapter Fourteen

STILLMAN CARESSED HIS Henry's hammer
as he put Sweets up the hill and under the portal straddling the trail leading into the Hollister
ranch headquarters. Just beyond the portal, he
stopped and looked around.

Horses milled in the three corrals to his left,
tails in the air, dust flying as a couple ran in cir-
cles around the corral, scenting the newcomer.
Sweets fidgeted and gave a deep-lunged whicker.
One of the horses in the corral whinnied in reply
and stopped to stare over the corral gate. Sweets
pranced, showing off.

There was another corral to Stillman's left—a
round breaking corral with a snubbing post
worn nearly clean through by all the riatas that
had been wrapped there over the thirty years
since Watt Hollister had built the place. A large
log barn and a slope-roofed side shed sat beyond

the corral. The bunkhouse, an L-shaped log affair with a shake-shingled roof and sagging front gallery, was a little farther away on the sheriff's left, beyond the corrals and stable.

The bunkhouse's wooden shutters were closed over most of the windows. Over the two glass windows flanking the closed front door, flour sack curtains were pulled back. Nothing moved behind the windows. At least, nothing that Stillman could see. No smoke rose from the large, adobe brick hearth running up the bunkhouse's far wall; nor did any rise from the tin chimney pipe likely venting a cook stove.

Seeing no one in the yard either, Stillman left his repeater at off-cock, the barrel resting across his saddle pommel, and booted Sweets on into the yard and around the large windmill and stone stock tank. A chaise with a black Morgan hitched to it sat in front of the main house's front veranda, the horse tied to the hitchrail.

As he drew up in front of the lodge, the front door latch clicked. Hinges squawked as the heavy door, constructed against possible Indian attacks, drew open. Old Watt Hollister came out and stepped onto the porch—a craggy-faced, gray-haired old man with a walrus mustache and a bleary look in his rheumy eyes. The way he seemed a little uncertain on his feet, swaying from side to side, Stillman thought he'd likely been drinking, which is what he'd heard he mainly did these days, leaving the running of the ranch to his sons and hired men, of which he had plenty.

Where were they now? Stillman had taken the fastest route out here from town, an old horse trail probably first blazed by Crow and Blackfeet hunting parties, not the wagon trail that Leon had probably taken with his rented wagon. The wagon trail was slower going, looping around hogbacks and bluffs. He'd doubted that he'd find his deputy on the trail, anyway. If he was anywhere, he was probably here—in one condition or another.

"Well, Sheriff Stillman . . ." Hollister said, drawing the heavy door closed behind him, giving a cordial nod. There'd been a dark, fateful pitch to his voice.

"My deputy make it out here with your daughter, Hollister?"

The old man nodded grimly as he shambled over to stand above the steps at the edge of the veranda. "Why, yes, he did. Yes, he did. Orlean is upstairs now, bein' tended by her mother and," he glanced at the chaise and the Morgan standing with one hip cocked, "and our dear neighbor, Mrs. Wolfram."

"My condolences for your loss," Stillman said. "I'm guessin' that Deputy McMannigle explained how it happened."

"Yes. Yes, he did. He said it was an accident. Happened quite by mistake." Hollister sighed and planted a large, gnarled hand on a porch post. "It wouldn't have happened at all if she'd stay home where she belonged . . . 'stead of runnin' around with long-loopin' desperadoes."

Stillman was a little confused by that. Her death had not been a mistake. She'd been trying to shoot him, Stillman, and his deputy had intervened. Anyway, the explanation didn't matter. What did matter was Leon.

"My deputy hasn't turned up back in Clantick, Mr. Hollister." Stillman had pitched his voice quite purposefully with accusation, lifting his head to glance at the lodge's upper story windows and then turning slightly to scrutinize the bunkhouse, which sat hunched and silent, the mid-afternoon's autumn sunlight bathing its shake roof in copper hues.

With his other hand, old Hollister twisted an end of his mustache. "Oh? That's odd."

"It is odd. What's odder is that his horse showed up without him and the wagon he was driving."

"Worrisome."

"He did leave here?"

"Oh, yes—he left here right after he dropped Orlean's body off. We're gettin' her ready for burial now. Probably bury her later today, maybe in the morning. Virginia is quite upset, as you can imagine."

Stillman looked at him curiously. Hollister met his gaze with a level, oblique one of his own. "How 'bout you? How are you holding up, Mr. Hollister?"

"About as well as you can imagine, Sheriff. I don't wear my emotions on my sleeve. But Orlean . . . well, she was my only daughter." Hollister glanced away, brushed a hand across his nose. "She was a good girl despite who she might have thrown in with. Certainly didn't deserve to die. She'd have come to her senses and come back to her family who loved her, but . . . well, that's not going to happen now."

He turned his sad, bitter gaze back to Stillman once more. "It's a bitter pill, Sheriff. But I'm workin' on swallowing it. It'll take time, but we'll move on without . . . without our daughter."

Stillman glanced around once more. "Where are your men, Mr. Hollister?"

Hollister glanced toward the bunkhouse and then shuttled his gaze to the corral where there were only a half-dozen or so horses milling. "I don't know. My sons handle all that. Probably down in the breaks, brush-popping any stubborn beeves they missed during roundup." He glanced at the sky. "Snow'll fly soon, most like."

Stillman looked around again in frustration. He'd found the old man convincing though doubt lingered. He supposed about the only thing he could do was take the wagon road to town and hope that he found Leon stalled somewhere with a broken axle, maybe. He might have unhitched the horse from the wagon, and the beast might have simply spooked and high-tailed it to town, stranding McMannigle in the mountains somewhere.

That didn't seem likely. Again, dread pinched the sheriff.

He looked at Hollister who was studying him with a faintly foxy look. The man didn't seem bitter enough over his daughter. He was hiding something. Only, Stillman couldn't bring himself to believe that such a well-to-do, longtime rancher would do anything to threaten his and his son's livelihoods, their sprawling, prosperous holdings out here in the Two-Bears.

That's exactly what he would have done if he'd murdered Leon. If that's what they'd done, they'd just incurred Stillman's wrath, and he'd by god burn their whole place to the ground so there wasn't enough left to haul away in a wheelbarrow.

Stillman narrowed an eye at the old rancher. "Hollister, I want to clarify something that my deputy in his good grace apparently left cloudy for you."

"What's that?"

"McMannigle shot your daughter because she'd been about to shoot me in the back. She was with two men, and she was as naked as the day she was born. I was fool enough to believe her story that she'd been taken hostage and turned my back on her. She pulled a gun on me, and she would have shot me if my deputy hadn't shot her first. That's how it happened, and I've written out an affidavit for the circuit judge and signed it."

Hollister's dark face turned crimson, all the warts and liver spots standing starkly out against it, as did his thick gray hair and mustache. He slowly raised his right arm and pointed a long, crooked finger at Stillman. His eyes blazed with unbridled fury. *That's a bald-faced lie!*

"That's bond," Stillman said mildly, backing his horse away from the veranda.

When he was even with the windmill and stock tank, he turned Sweets around and galloped under the portal and down the slope toward the creek. Behind him, he heard Hollister's phlegmy voice peel like thunder. *That's a bald-faced lie!*

~~~

"What do you think, Doc?" Evelyn Vincent asked Evans as the doctor came down the steep stairs in his house. She'd been waiting in the parlor for him while he'd examined Tommy Dilloughboy in the room he used for overnight patients.

The stocky Evans, dressed in his usual shabby suit minus the jacket, removed his stethoscope from around his neck and ran a thick hand through his unruly mop of dark-red hair. His round-rimmed spectacles, which gave his crooked-nosed, roughhewn face—the face of a man who'd put himself through medical school by boxing with his bare knuckles—flashed in the light of the parlor windows.

"Oh, I think he'll be fine. Right fine. Not to worry, Evelyn." The doctor clutched her arm affectionately and planted a kiss on her forehead. "He has the best sawbones in the territory, don't ya know." He chuckled wryly and started for the kitchen. "He lost some blood, but he's a strapping young man. He'll get his strength back in no time. Probably be able to walk out of here tomorrow, in fact."

"Is there anything I can do for him, Doc?"

Evans stopped in the parlor doorway, wrinkling the skin above the bridge of his nose. "Evelyn, isn't this the young fella I saw you walking around town with last spring?"

Her cheeks warming, Evelyn glanced at her hands which she'd nervously entwined before her belly. She'd dreaded this part of the conversation, which she'd anticipated.

The doctor continued with, "And he isn't he the same one who Ben ran out of town when he heard about the younker's plans to rob the Drovers Saloon?"

"One and the same, Doc," Evelyn said with a sigh, turning down her mouth corners. "It's true, he got into some trouble last summer, and Ben told him to leave and not return for a year, but . . . but, Doc, what was I supposed to do? He was out there in the cold night, *wounded . . . ?*"

"How was he wounded? Who shot him?"

"Apparently, someone was trying to steal his horse. Drygulched him!"

Evans appeared to consider that skeptically. "Drygulched him, huh?"

"Yep."

"Well . . ."

"Doc, you won't tell Ben he's here, will you? Before Tommy agreed to come and see you, he made me promise that you wouldn't tell Ben."

Evans raked a finger down his mustache and goatee, which were the same dark-red as his hair and flecked with crumbs from a sandwich he'd apparently eaten earlier. Evelyn had just come over from Sam Wa's Café, taking a break after preparing for the supper crowd, to check on Tommy Dilloughboy. She hadn't lingered here last night after she'd brought Tommy over and turned him over to the doc, because she hadn't wanted to answer the very questions the doctor had posed to her now.

"Well, now, that sounds a might suspicious to me, Evelyn."

"I reckon it does to me, as well," she said with another fateful sigh. But then she gave the sawbones another look of beseeching. "Doc, I really think that deep down Tommy's a good sort. I think, being half-Indian an' all, he's had a tough life. I know as well as anyone that having a tough life can lead you to make some bad decisions. But I think if he's treated kindly, and helped . . . and trusted—well, I just think it sure couldn't hurt. I can't blame Ben, but he's a lawman, Doc. And you know how lawmen are."

"Yes, I know. They can be quite intransigent sometimes."

"They can be right *what?*" Evelyn was always amused as well as mystified by the doctor's vocabulary. She admired him terribly, and she had to admit that she rather fancied him, but now, with Tommy having ridden back into her life, she realized that the gulf between her and the educated sawbones encompassed more than just years. He could never feel toward her, a simple working girl, anything close to how she felt toward him.

"Uh . . . sorry," the doc said, looking sheepish. "What I mean is they can be rather stubborn at times. Ben has done a good job of cleaning up this town in the two years since he's been here, and he takes pride in keeping it that way. Can't blame him."

"I certainly don't, but . . ." She looked at the doctor from under her brows.

"But your secret's safe with me. I figure what Ben doesn't know can't hurt him, though I don't think young Mr. Dilloughboy best linger in Clantick overlong unless he wants to wind up in the calboose."

"No, I suppose not."

"Don't look so long-faced, Evelyn. I can see how a young lady might be attracted to my bright-eyed and bushy-tailed patient up there. But rest assure there are other, better fish in the sea."

Evelyn knew that was true. And she cursed herself for having gotten so entangled with Tommy. Especially since she doubted that he felt as strongly about her as she did about him. Wasn't that just her fate, though—to always be tumbling for the wrong men?

"I know you're right, Doc. In the meantime, is it all right if I go up and see him?"

"Sure. Why don't you swab his forehead a few times? I've left a bowl of water and a cloth up there. We're going to need to get his temperature down, though I think it's already on the wane."

"You got it, Doc."

"As for me," Evans said, cupping a hand to his ear. "I hear a brandy calling me from the kitchen."

"Awfully early, Doc," Evelyn gently admonished.

"You sound like Katherine," he grumbled and turned away.

"Doc?"

"Yay-up?"

"Thanks."

The stocky, handsome pill roller shrugged and crooked his mouth then turned and strode off toward the kitchen and his brandy bottle and likely a fat cigar and the several piles of books he kept on his table which he read all night long. Evelyn would have felt lonesome for him, though his lonesomeness—if he was lonesome, he'd never mentioned it to her and she considered them fairly close friends and confidants—would soon end.

Soon, he and the Widow Kemmett would marry.

Evelyn sighed as she climbed the steep stairs to the doctor's creaky second story. It wouldn't be long before the whole world had paired up and gotten married.

The whole world, that was, except for Evelyn Vincent. She'd be the only one left alone.

"There she is," said Tommy Dilloughboy as Evelyn tapped once on his half-open door and poked her head into the room. "There's the prettiest girl in the whole, gallblasted world!"

Chapter Fifteen

"WAIT A MINUTE." LEON sat up on the cot and wrapped his left hand around the girl's right wrist before she could touch the wet cloth again to his leg. "You're Hollister's wife?"

Her eyes were strangely innocent. She looked up at him as though she didn't think there was anything even faintly ironic about the information she'd just given him.

"Yes."

McMannigle scowled at her, his lower jaw hanging.

The disbelief must have been plain in his eyes, because she smiled and said, "Oh, I know what you're thinkin'. You're thinkin' ain't it odd for Nash's wife to be dressin' your wound for you. Oh, I bet you didn't even know Nash was married." She laughed. "That's all right. Nash acts like he don't even know most of the time himself!"

She dabbed at the bloody hole again. "And I reckon you'd be right about it bein' odd, me helpin' you . . . if I was the sort of person who could sit around and watch an innocent man be killed when I had a chance to help him. You see, I seen you from my bedroom window in the house. I spend a lot of time up there, you understand. I don't fit in all that well with the family, especially with Virginia Hollister. She don't like it that her boy married me, so I don't go down much. I'm just in the way, anyway, and the old man—well, he looks at me strange. I've caught him peakin' through the keyhole in the door to me and Nash's room when I've been takin' a bath. Ain't that the most disgusting thing you ever heard? Sinful old codger!"

She wrung the rag out in the pan again and set the pan on the floor.

"No, I was just sittin' there in the window, thinkin' about goin' for a ride—ridin' my horse, Biscuit, is my favorite thing to do; that and writing poetry in my journal—when I seen you ride up on Blaze Westin's horse. Why in the world did you come back here of all places?"

"I reckon Westin's horse was homesick."

"The old man and Carlton Ramsay are drinking toddies in the parlor, and Virginia's upstairs with Zeb and Mrs. Wolfram, so no one seen you. That was close, though, for sure. You're lucky Barney's off huntin' rabbits or somesuch!" She laughed darkly. "All the men are out—well, they're out lookin' for you, but I reckon you know that better than anybody."

"Yeah, I know that pretty well."

"I'm going to splash some whiskey on that wound so I can sew it closed. If I sew it closed without cleanin' it out real good, it's like to putrefy and you could lose your leg."

Leon was looking out the one window from which the shutter was drawn back. The light had faded considerably; it felt like afternoon. "What time is it, anyway?"

"I don't know—around three, maybe. I had to leave you for a while after I got you in here. Had to fetch the whiskey and my sewing pouch from the cabin. Told old Watt I was takin' Biscuit for a ride. When I got here, you were so sound asleep, I just let you sleep. I knew you needed it, and I got time to kill."

"Are your husband and his men back yet?"

"They weren't when I went back. You ready?"

Leon looked at the bottle she was holding up as though threatening him with it.

"Ah, Jesus—yeah, go ahead."

She lowered the bottle, turned it, let the whiskey splash over the ragged, red hole that she'd done a fine job of cleaning. The busthead hit the deputy's leg like liquid fire. It drove a bayonet of agony into the wound, up through his groin and into his belly where it twisted around demonically, flaring even more vigorously.

McMannigle gritted his teeth, stiffened his neck, and arched his back, dug his heels—she'd removed his boots—into the log frame at the bottom of the cot.

"Ay, yi, yi . . . yi—that hurt pretty good, all right!"

"I'm sorry," she said, smiling sweetly, with genuine regret.

"No need. I do thank ya mighty kindly, Mrs. Hollister."

"Call me Carrie Anne. That's my name."

"Thank you mighty kindly, Carrie Anne." The pain subsided, and as she corked the bottle, he said, "Carrie Anne, why in the hell are you doin' this, anyway? Your husband tried to kill me and now here you are--hidin' me out on his ranch, doctorin' my wound . . ."

She stood and moved to a table that abutted the one-room cabin's front wall and retrieved a small burlap pouch. "What's wrong is wrong, Deputy. Deep down, Nash knows it. Deep down, even old Watt knows it. They did a devilish thing in tryin' to kill you." She'd stopped after she turned away from the table and looked down at the pouch in her hands. "I hope . . . well, I hope you can find a way to forgive them."

She looked at Leon, her eyes searching his. She was beautiful. Her waifish, round-faced, hazel-eyed innocence accentuated her beauty. She had a small mole on the otherwise smooth line of her jaw. Her face was lightly tanned, likely from riding in the open air. Her eyes were as deep and luminous as fresh spring water.

McMannigle had never heard about her before; he'd had no idea Nash Hollister was even married, let alone hitched to this innocent, frank-eyed, earthy country girl who loved to ride her horse and write poetry. And who was obviously an alien here.

"Do you think you can forgive him, Mr. Mc-Mannigle?"

"I don't know," Leon said as she continued walking toward him. "I reckon I can work on it."

Forgive them? Would they forgive him if they found him here?

Would they forgive *her* for helping him . . . ?

The deputy wondered if she realized the danger in the game she was playing. If it wasn't for her, though, he'd be dead about now.

"Best take a sip of that," she said, handing him the bottle as she pulled the chair closer to the bed, and sat down on it.

"Just a sip?" McMannigle gave an ironic snort and took a long pull. When he had that one down and it was working on him, soothing him, dulling the throb in his thigh, he took another and then one more. He felt so much better that he set the bottle down beside him on the cot, cradling it proprietarily in his arm. "Don't mind if I hold onto it, do you?"

"No, you go ahead. You'll likely need more of it, but you'd best not drink too much on an empty stomach, or you'll get sick." She was holding a needle up to the fading window light, frowning as she threaded the needle with catgut.

"You know what I think?" she asked when she'd threaded the needle and had sat down in the chair angled toward the cot.

"What's that?"

"I think everything's gonna be just fine. Trouble passes. You know, I've always believed that, and believing in that one simple thing has gotten me through a lot of hard times. It's kept me here in that big house with old Watt and Miss Virginia and her Bible though Nash keeps promisin' that he's going to build us our own cabin right over here next to this one. We'll use this little cabin for storage, though that'd sorta be a shame."

She glanced around, that dreamy smile still quirking her lips. "If these walls could talk." She chuckled, and her hazel eyes sparkled prettily. "This is where me and Nash started out. I met him out on the range. My pa's ranch was down in the Missouri River breaks. That was before he got sick and died. But I'd sneak up here to see Nash on the sly—you know, so Miss Virginia never found out—and we'd meet up here for some wild times."

Something caught her eye in the corner over Leon's right shoulder. "Ah . . . look there." She reached over him and removed from a small, corner shelf a brass ambrotype case. She wiped cobwebs from the case, flipped the tiny latch, and opened the cover. "Oh, my gosh."

Leon took another pull from the bottle. He wanted to be good and soused when she started suturing the bullet hole closed. "What is it?"

Carrie Anne sniffed, smeared a tear on her cheek with the back of her hand. "They sat for a photograph." She turned the open case toward Leon, revealing a hand-tinted oval photograph showing a dark-skinned young man with thick, wavy brown hair and a soot-smudge mustache sitting on a chair with a girl standing beside him in a simple cream taffeta dress with lace on the sleeves and collar, a cameo pin holding the collar closed at her throat.

She held a small bouquet of what appeared

wildflowers in her hands. The girl had her head tilted to one side, smiling serenely. She wore her hair braided and wound atop her head and also flowing down her slender shoulders. She looked like a springtime maiden from a fairy tale. The young man looked deadly serious and a little uncomfortable in his shabby, ill-fitting suit, but there was still a wry light in his dark-brown eyes that were shiny from the photographer's flash powder.

Leon returned his gaze to the thin, pale, delicately featured girl who wore her hair in braids wrapped around the top of her head, smiling so sweetly, hopefully at the camera. The smile was in such contrast from the expression Leon had seen on her face just before he'd shot her that his guts clenched.

There was a thickness in the deputy's throat. He cleared it, said, "Miss . . . Orlean?"

Carrie Anne turned the photograph back toward her. "And her fiancé, Tommy Dilloughboy." Lowering the ambrotype case, she glanced pensively around the shabby cabin. "They met here . . . just like me and Nash did. I seen 'em. A coupla times. I was out ridin' and I spied their horses here. I shouldn't have watched," she smeared another couple of more tears on her cheeks, "but I did. They were so in love, havin' so much fun, just like me an' Nash once did--years ago, now! Right down there on this very same cot . . . in this shabby old cabin."

Leon glanced over his shoulder at the shelf, saw several burned down candles lined up there on the lids of airtight tins and a box of stove matches. There was also a small, pale, oval-shaped object. A sheepskin pregnancy sheath, most likely. The deputy rolled his eyes to glance down at the cot, feeling a little self-conscious suddenly, as though he'd invaded an intimate place, which he reckoned he had.

"Tommy Dilloughboy," he said, frowning at Carrie Anne. "He . . ."

"Worked for Nash and old Watt. When Watt caught Orlean and Tommy moonin' around together, he got suspicious and ordered Tommy off the ranch. Miss Virginia went after poor Orlean with a wooden spoon right out in the yard for all to see. That night, Orlean left. I begged her not to. Me an' Orlean were like sisters . . . I loved her . . . so enjoyed her spirit brightening up that dingy old house . . . but she couldn't bear another minute. It was like prison to her . . . just like it is to me, I reckon. The only reason I can stand it is because I know Nash is gonna build us our own lodge right here in this hollow—away from old Watt's lusty peeks and Miss Virginia and that

Bible's she's always walkin' around the house, recitin' . . .."

She let her voice trail off.

McMannigle's mind was in a complicated knot. Carrie Anne. Orlean. Tommy Dilloughboy. Nash and his men. He couldn't work through the mess because of the pain in his leg and the whiskey he'd been drinking.

Really, what he mostly wanted to do right now was sleep. His eyelids were getting heavy.

"There, that's good," Carrie Anne said. "You're gettin' sleepy. You just go to sleep, and I'll stitch that hole in your leg. Then I'll try to fetch you some food from the cabin."

"Don't do nothin' dangerous, Carrie Anne," Leon heard himself say from far away, the warm tendrils of sleep reaching up to take him. "Don't do nothin' to get yourself caught . . . helpin' the devil who killed Orlean. Likely wouldn't go . . . too well for you."

"Don't you worry," the girl said, her voice sort of revolving distantly around him, as if she were calling down from the top of that well again. "Everything's gonna be just fine. I know it is. I'm a strong believer in certain things, and I just know everything's gonna turn out just fine. We're all gonna live happily ever after. Except for . . . Orlean, of course . . .."

Leon thought he heard the girl choke back a sob.

Chapter Sixteen

EVELYN COULD FEEL her whole face light up, ears warming, as she walked into the small room with a dormer window and a single, small bed beside a marble-topped washbasin and with the handsome Tommy Dilloughboy lying under the bedcovers, grinning up at her from where his handsome, brown-haired head lay deep in a snowy white pillow.

"How're you doing, Tommy? The doc says you're on the mend."

"I feel like I'm on the mend." The young man's darkly tanned cheeks dimpled as he smiled, and his brown eyes flashed warmly. "Thanks to you."

He patted the bed beside him, urging her to sit.

"Thanks to Doc Evans, you mean," Evelyn said, happily obliging the boy by sitting down beside him on the edge of the bed. She leaned over him and placed her hand on his forehead.

"You're warm, all right. Doc said you still have a temperature though he don't sound too worried about it."

"My thermometer just started climbin' when I seen you walk into the room." He grinned, showing that chipped front tooth that made him look like a precious though devilish young schoolboy.

Tommy placed his hands on her arms, drew her down to him, and kissed her gently, sweetly.

"Now, Tommy," Evelyn said with mock admonishing because she didn't think anything in the world tasted as good as Tommy's lips, "you best not let yourself get all het up. You got a bullet hole in your side, young man!"

But she did not resist when he drew her head down to his once more and placed his lips more firmly against hers. She returned the kiss, enjoying the warmth of his mouth, the masculine smell of him beneath the medicinal smell of the arnica and the poultice that the doctor had placed over his wound.

But when she tried to pull away, he tightened his grip on her arms, holding her against him.

"Tommy," she said.

"Why don't you climb on in here?"

"What?" She chuckled. "No!"

He kissed her again. She had to admit that his hand felt good, but this was neither the time nor the place.

She pulled her head away from his. "Tommy, no."

"Remember last summer?" he said. "Down in that old stable by the river?"

"How could I forget? But we're not down by the river, and we're not alone."

"Ah, hell, I bet the ole sawbones is three sheets to the wind by now. I've heard his reputation for drink . . . and ladies. He's right handsome, ain't he?"

"I don't know. I guess."

"I hear he's got credit down at Mrs. Lee's place." Mrs. Lee ran the most respectable brothel in Clantick.

"I wouldn't know about that." Now she thought she could smell—and taste—more than just medicine. She thought she could taste whiskey on the young man's breath. "Tommy, have you been drinking?"

"Sure. I have a lot of pain, Evelyn. The doc gave me a few snorts. Said it's the same as laudanum." He canted his head slightly to one side, studying Evelyn dubiously. "You like that old sawbones, don't you?"

"What? Why would you--?"

"I don't know—just somethin' in the way you two was talkin' last night. I heard you talkin' downstairs earlier, too. Tell me, you ever . . .?" He raised and lowered his browed lasciviously.

"Of course not! The doc's going to marry the Widow Kemmett soon!"

"Bet he'd rather have you than some dried up old widow." Tommy squeezed her bosom harder until it no longer felt so good. "You ever show him these?" He gritted his teeth, and there was a hard, cold light that she'd never seen before in his eyes. It was almost as though he'd suddenly donned a mask that looked much like him but with hard, cold devils' eyes.

Feeling the heat of anger now, Evelyn stiffened and pulled away from him. "Tommy, you let me go! I don't like what you just said. I don't like it one blame bit!"

He laughed suddenly. Just as suddenly, his eyes were the old Tommy's again, deep and dreamy and vaguely almond-shaped. "Ah, I'm sorry, Evelyn. I didn't mean no harm. I reckon I just been up here all day thinkin' about you and . . . well, *us* . . . and I just started gettin' a little jealous is all, wonderin' what you been up to . . . who you been seein' . . . since I pulled out of town. I'm sorry. That was just the doc's whiskey talkin'. I should know better than to . . ."

He let his voice trail off. His eyes grew opaque, as though he were staring right through her. He was listening to something outside. Evelyn heard it, too—the thudding of many horses. The thuds were growing quickly louder.

Evelyn said, "What on earth?" She crouched to look out the dormer window. With a painful grunt, Tommy turned himself around in bed to peer out the window, as well. The window faced southeast, in the direction of town. Several horseback riders were just then galloping up the trail that climbed the bluff that the doctor's sprawling, old house was perched on.

More than several.

As the line of riders grew as they rose up from over the side of the bluff and galloped toward the house, Evelyn estimated there must have been a good dozen or more.

"Oh, my gosh," Evelyn said. "Why do you suppose all those men are--?"

"Ah, Christ!" Tommy threw his covers back and, wincing and holding a hand over the poultice bandaged over the bullet wound, dropped his legs to the floor. He leaned closer to the window, staring down at the riders just now lining out in front of the doctor's house.

Evelyn stared at Tommy, befuddled. "Tommy, what . . . ?"

"Get back!" he ordered, grabbing her arm and pulling her back away from the window, letting the curtain drop back into place.

Evelyn heard the doctor's footsteps on the floor downstairs. He'd apparently heard the riders and was going to the front door.

Evelyn looked out the window again, saw that all the riders were holding rifles. They were all dressed in the rough trail garb, including chaps and buckskin jackets and buffeting scarves of cow waddies. Ranchmen.

The lead rider was tall and dark with a brushy mustache mantling his grim mouth. He wore a high-crowned, gray Stetson and a red scarf under the collar of his buckskin coat. As he swung down from the saddle of his large dun, he turned back toward the men and told them something that Evelyn couldn't hear above Tommy's heavy breathing and the pounding of the doctor's shoes on the first-story floor. Evelyn could only hear the deep, business-like rumble of the man's voice.

"Tommy, who is that?" Evelyn turned to see that the young man, wearing only his faded red long handles and black wool socks, had gone to the chair sitting against the opposite wall from the bed. His clothes were draped over the chair, and his cartridge belt and holster hung from a spool of the chair's back.

He unsnapped the thong from over his gun's hammer and slid the gun from its holster.

"Tommy, what on earth is going on?" Evelyn demanded, tightening her jaws as well as her voice.

He turned to her, and his face was a mask

of anxiety. Veins forked in his forehead, over his right eye. Both eyes were sharp, his sweaty cheeks crimson. "You stay here!" He motioned to her angrily. "Just stay here, Evelyn! Don't make a sound—understand?"

"Tommy, I want to--"

"Shut up and do as I tell you, damnit!"

The harsh tone of his voice rocked the girl back on her heels. She watched, stricken, as he opened the door and, moving on the balls of his stocking feet, walked into the hall, turned right, and dropped nearly soundlessly down the stairs. Evelyn could hear the steps creaking under his weight. At the same time, she heard the downstairs door open, and men's voices, including Doc Evans'.

Too curious to follow Tommy's orders, Evelyn hurried into the hall and looked down the stairs. Tommy was nowhere in sight.

Quietly, Evelyn slipped down the stairs, holding the rail with one hand and running her other palm across the opposite wall, trying to lighten her tread on the stairs. She moved into the parlor and stopped when she saw Tommy standing beside the parlor's open French doors. He had his cocked revolver in one hand, and he was standing tensely, canting his head to listen to Doc Evans saying, ". . . why are you all looking for him, anyway? Say, what's all this about, Hollister?"

Nash Hollister: Evelyn thought she'd recognized the lead rider. She'd seen the Hollisters in town from time to time though they never dined at Sam Wa's humble café but at the Boston House Hotel and Restaurant. That's where most of the mucky-mucks dined.

"Just answer the question, Doc," the brusque oldest Hollister son demanded in a menacingly level tone. "Is he here or have you seen him?"

"No, he isn't here, and I haven't seen him," Evans said, his voice more muffled because he was facing away from the house. "Now, kindly tell me why you're looking for him. What's this all--"

"You mind if we come in and take a look around?"

Tommy shook his head. Evelyn heard him suck air through his teeth. He hadn't seen her standing behind him, at the bottom of the stairs. He was too intent on what was happening at the front door.

Evelyn gave a silent gasp as the young man began raising his cocked revolver and extending it through the open French doors toward the doctor's dingy foyer from which the men's muffled voices echoed woodenly.

"Yes, I do mind. And I got a shotgun that minds, as well," Evans said. "Now, you got a good dozen men. I understand that. Which one or two do you want filled with twelve-gauge buckshot?"

Despite her nervousness and exasperation, Evelyn had to give a thin smile at the doc's pluck.

No one said anything for a while. Tommy was aiming his revolver straight through the open French doors and through a dim, little vestibule that the doctor used for a closet—a cluttered, musty closet, at that--toward the foyer opening beyond it. Every muscle in his back stood out in sharp relief beneath his tight long handle shirt.

"All right, all right," Hollister said. "We'll take your word the deputy ain't here, Doc. Where do you suppose Stillman is? We went by the jail-house and it was closed for business."

"I couldn't tell you where either of them are," Evans said.

"You're just real helpful today—ain't ya, Doc?" said a more distant voice than Hollister's. It probably belonged to one of the men sitting their horses in the doc's yard.

"Who is that—Sandy Wilkes?" Evans said, raising his voice. "Sandy, you'd better hope you don't dislocate your shoulder again like you did last fall, 'cause you'll be looking for some other sawbones to snap it back into place for you."

A couple of the other men chuckled.

"All right, Doc—we get the drift," Hollister said. "Go back to your busthead and your books. We'll be on our way. Oh, and, uh . . . pardon the interruption."

Evans said forthrightly and not without a touch of irony, "Nash, I just hope to god your intentions are honorable—whatever they are. I have no idea why you're looking for Stillman and McMannigle, but this town and county holds them both in high regard. You remember that."

Boots thumped on the porch and then Evelyn heard Nash descend the porch steps, his voice lower now as he said, "Thanks for the advice, Doc. I'll remember it, for sure. Just wanna have a little chat—that's all. Nothin' to get your back in a hump over."

There was another silence. Evelyn saw Tommy's shoulder blades smooth out against his back, behind his underwear top. From beyond him, she could hear tack squawking and then men clucking to their horses and the thudding of hooves as the Triple H Connected riders started riding away. Evans closed the door with a latching click, muttering to himself, "Little chat, my ass. With a dozen armed riders?"

Tommy turned away from the French doors and froze when he saw Evelyn. "Hey," the young man whispered as Evans's shoes thumped in the foyer. "I thought I told you to stay upstairs."

"I don't take orders from you, Tommy Dilloughboy. What have you gotten yourself into? Why were you thinkin' those Triple H Connected riders were after you?"

Before Tommy could respond, Evans said from the foyer, "Evelyn—that you?"

Tommy cast an anxious gaze behind him and then rushed passed Evelyn, giving her the stink-eye, and then hurried on up the stairs to his room. Evelyn had returned his look, and now she stood in the foyer, arms crossed on her chest, anger burning through her.

She'd trusted that boy, but he'd lied to her. She didn't know what the lie was exactly, but he'd gotten himself in trouble again. Possibly trouble out at the Triple H Connected where he'd worked until, according to him, he'd been routinely turned loose after the autumn gather.

Evans stopped in the door to the foyer, peering into the parlor beyond the vestibule. "Evelyn?"

"Yeah, I'm here, Doc."

He hooked his thumb toward the front door. "Did you hear that?"

"I heard."

"They were looking for Leon. And Ben, too, but it sounds like the trouble starts with Leon. You know where he and Ben are off to?" He frowned, cocked his head a little. "Are you all right, girl? You look a little peaked."

"I'm just a little perplexed, is all."

"About them?" Evans asked, turning his head toward the front door.

"About life in general, I reckon. Including them." She walked toward Evans, her concern now shifting from Tommy Dilloughboy to Ben and Leon. "Doc, Ben rode out of town this morning like a mule with tin cans tied to its tail. He said he was gonna look for Leon out at the Triple H Connected. He was in such a hurry, he didn't tell me much—only said I was deputized."

"You? *Deputized?*"

Evelyn slapped a hand over her mouth. "That reminds me—I best check on Ben's prisoners, build up the fire in the wood stove over there. I gotta go, Doc." She patted the sawbones' shoulder, saw the concerned look in his bespectacled eyes, and paused. "What do you suppose that's all about Doc? You think Ben and Leon have trouble with the Triple H Connected?"

"Sure as hell sounds like it."

"It does, doesn't it?" Evelyn cast her peeved, indignant gaze toward the ceiling. "Trouble. Seems to be a lot of it these days."

Chapter Seventeen

STILLMAN KICKED THE big man's body onto its back and saw the two brown eyes staring up at him from a broad, savage face.

Long, straight brown hair curled against the man's scarred, pitted cheeks that, while naturally ruddy, were turning pasty with death. Blood stained the front of the man's shirt and vest. It was dusk, and it was cool, but the day's last flies buzzed around the blood staining the ground as well as the dead man himself. A light breeze jostled his long mares' tail mustaches.

A big devil. Probably Mexican. Stillman thought he'd seen the savage, pockmarked face on a wanted dodger or two hanging in his office. Hiring known killers with paper on their heads meant that old Watt Hollister wasn't as upstanding as Stillman had once thought.

The sheriff inspected the ground to the right

of the dead man. Dirt and gravel were badly scuffed. The dirt and short, brown grass and dried up wildflowers showed where someone had lain flat not all that long ago. At least, sometime in the past twenty-four hours. Not the big Mexican. Stillman could see where he'd fallen, and he'd pretty much lain right there, not moving around much if any. Whoever had killed him had been lying here in wait. There was a smear of blood about the size of Stillman's palm beside where the second man had lain.

The second man had been wounded.

Leon?

Stillman took a deep draught of air that burned in his throat and lungs like a dragon's breath. He'd seen the wagon parked beside the clearing. He'd seen the remains of the campfire and his deputy's gear strewn beside it. There was a dead man in the creek, three more on the slope above the creek, another one—the Triple H Connected foreman, Blaze Westin—lying dead on the crest of the ridge.

And there was this man here.

As yet, Stillman had not found Leon.

The light was fading quickly. It would be good dark within the hour. He had to keep looking, hoping to pick up his deputy's trail.

On the other side of the ridge, Sweets whinnied long and shrilly--a warning whinnie. Close on the heels of his bay's alarm, hooves thudded farther off in the distance. He could hear a man's distance-muffled shout.

Stillman hefted his Henry, pushed through the screen of pine branches, and began climbing the steep slope toward the bluff's crest. As his boots slipped on the sharp incline, he pushed off the ground with his free left hand, grunting and panting with the effort. More shouting rose from the other side of the ridge.

Again, Sweets whinnied his shrill warning. Breathless, Stillman gained the crest of the ridge and dropped to hands and knees, peering into the valley on the other side.

Sweets stood ground-reined near Leon's cold fire ring. The bay was fidgeting and tossing his head as he looked toward the dozen or so riders galloping toward him from the direction of the wagon trail. The riders were spread out in a long line.

Some were sliding carbines from rifle scabbards. Others already had their rifles in their hands. Some were pumping cartridges into firing chambers. Though the light was a yellowish-amber dusky murk, Stillman recognized the mustached rider astraddle a clean-lined dun at the prow of the bow-shaped group. The fast-fading light from the west touched Nash Hollister's left cheek and the crown of his hat.

Suddenly feeling like a fox with a party of Englishmen and their blooded hounds honing in on him, Stillman bit off a glove, stuck two fingers between his lips, and whistled loudly. Sweets bucked eagerly, swung around, gave his rear hooves an angry kick, and galloped across the creek before lunging up the slope nearly directly below Stillman.

The fading light flashed lemon-gray on the anxious horse's eyes as, trailing his reins, which bounced and leaped around his scissoring legs, the horse pounded up the slope. Below and beyond him, the riders now closing on the camp started shouting louder. A few triggered their rifles, which flashed fire and expelled smoke, the slugs spanging off rocks or breaking branches behind and around Stillman's thundering bay.

Stillman shouted, "Hey, you shoot my horse, I'll blow you to Kingdom Come, you sons of devils!"

At the same time, he racked a cartridge into his Henry's breech, aimed down the slope over Sweet's bouncing, curving bulk, and fired. He didn't have a clear shot through the darkening trees, but he thought he saw several riders hesitate. And then Sweets was pounding within eight feet of the ridge crest, and Stillman leaped to his feet, grabbed the reins, and swung into the saddle.

"He-yahhh, boy!"

The horse galloped on across the top of the ridge and down the other side, Stillman holding the reins up high against his chest in one hand, extending his big Henry out for balance in his other hand. The bay plunged down the slope, hammering his front hooves into the steeply pitched ground with each lunge, Stillman leaning far back over his cantle to keep from being thrown over the bay's head.

Behind him he heard Watt Hollister shout, "Keep goin' boys! Get that son of a buck!"

Stillman had little doubt the shooters knew who he was. They'd been hunting somebody, likely his deputy, McMannigle, but now their sights had swung toward him, and they hadn't hesitated before giving chase. Something told him that the fact he was wearing a badge wasn't going to deter them in the least.

If you've killed one lawman, you might as well kill two. A man can hang only once.

This was war.

Stillman stopped Sweets at the bottom of the hill and leaped out of the saddle. He winced at a sharp ache in his back—the flare-up of the bullet lodged within a hair's breadth of his spine. An old injury. One he'd been told he'd have to deal with sooner rather than later but one that he'd been putting off now with Faith pregnant. As he dropped down behind a low hummock of ground, he hoped it didn't impede him here.

Holding Sweets's reins in his left hand, he shouldered the Henry and gazed up the darkening slope. The dozen or so riders had crested the bluff and were making it down toward him, still spread out in a long, ragged line through the pine trees stippling the bluff's steep shoulder. A couple were taking shots at him, their bullets landing several yards short or wide.

Stillman racked another round into the Henry's breech, slid the rifle to his right, tracking and aiming about seventy yards up the slope, and fired. The horse of his target screeched shrilly, dropped to its knees, and rolled. The rider's own scream was clipped by the horse's plunge on top of him.

As the horse gained its feet, saddle hanging askew, its wounded rider flopped around, writhing and groaning.

Stillman aimed again, fired again, and felt the satisfaction of watching his second target tumble straight back over his horse's arched tail and disappearing from view as the horse, apparently not knowing its rider had met his demise, kept running nearly straight down the slope. Stillman aimed again, fired again, and curled his mouth corners as a shouted epithet hurled toward him. His third target dropped his rifle, grabbed his left shoulder, and sagged forward over his horse's pole.

Two seconds later, he tumbled off his mount's left stirrup, gone from Stillman's view though the sheriff could hear him thrashing and snapping brush.

Stillman had not fired the third shot before a voice he recognized as Nash Hollister's started shouting loudly, "Hold up! Hold up! *Retreat . . . or he'll pick us off with that damn Henry of his like turkeys on fence posts!*"

Most of the last light was gone and stars were shimmering in the velvet sky touched with lilac, but Stillman could see the silhouettes of the Triple H Connected men as they whipped their horses around and headed back up the side of the bluff, meandering around trees, the horses grunting like blacksmiths' bellows as they dug their hooves in and lunged.

Hooves thudded and tack squawked and men grunted angrily and cursed.

The riders disappeared into the darkness at the top of the bluff.

Stillman waited, caressing his Henry's cocked hammer.

He waited some more. Silence grew as the air chilled, the temperature dropping fast.

"Stillman!" called Nash Hollister, his voice sounding hollow and oddly close in the vast, starry night. "Stillman, that you down there?"

Stillman angrily brushed his forearm across his mustache and narrowed his eyes. "It ain't Santa Clause, Hollister, you son of a buck! Where's my deputy? Where's McMannigle?"

"He's dead! Or just as good as. Same as you, Stillman!"

Stillman ground his back teeth. "Why don't you come down here and try to make good on your threat, you yellow-livered coward!"

He waited for Hollister's reply. It didn't come for nearly a minute, and when it did, the eldest Hollister son's voice lacked its previous bravado. It was conciliatory, even chagrined. "Look, damnit, Stillman—I ain't the one that brung it to this!"

"Who did?"

"I was followin' the old man's orders. That Negro deputy of yours killed my sister, so you can understand how we was all upset about it. All right, we didn't think it through. You try thinkin' it through in a similar situation."

Stillman scowled, not quite able to believe what he was hearing.

"I know we shouldn't have lit out after him, but we did. I know he's wounded and he's on foot somewhere out here. Likely dead. I wish things could be different, and I reckon they could be if you'd just agree to forget about it, but I reckon you wouldn't be game for that--would you?"

"Game for forgetting that you murdered my deputy in cold blood? No, I don't think I'd be game for that, Nash."

"That's what I figured. And I understand. Say, Stillman?"

"What?"

"We was just in town earlier. Smashed hell out of the telegraph key in the Wells Fargo office, in case you get it in mind to ride back to town and invite more lawmen to our little fandango out here. Also told the telegrapher, Mr. Mitchell, about what would happen if he sent any telegrams off to, say, the U.S. Marshal down in Helena. You know, with any mentions of the Triple H Connected in 'em. I do believe he got the drift. Yessir. Anyways, it don't really matter. I doubt he'll be able to get another key for at least two weeks. One would probably have to be shipped out from Chicago or St. Paul, most like."

Stillman laughed darkly. "So, you're goin' all the way with this—eh, Nash?"

"What choice do I have?"

Stillman off-cocked his rifle, rose, and, wincing at the creak in his back, grabbed his horse's saddlehorn. "You could choose a trial, risk a hangin'." He swung up into the leather, almost certain that the darkness concealed him down here.

"Or I could just kill you, make sure your deputy's dead. Pains me to say it, it genuinely does, though I know that's a little tough to believe. But it really does, Stillman. I'm not a born killer. It's just a tough situation, that's all."

"You have my sympathy." Stillman neck-reined Sweets away from the bluff and touched spurs to the horse's flanks. Glancing over his left shoulder, he yelled, "You just remember that before I pull a bullet through your no-account head, you chicken-hearted son of a devil! Both you and old Watt! You remember that!"

Stillman turned his head forward and touched steel again to Sweets's flanks.

"After him, boys!" Hollister shouted from the top of the bluff. "Whoever drills him first gets double pay!"

At the risk of breaking both his and his horse's neck, Stillman put Sweets into a full gallop through a crease in the buttes, heading generally south. His plan was to lead them all into the southern Two-Bears and kill them one-by-one and two-by-two.

Chapter Eighteen

CARRIE ANNE ENTERED the Hollister lodge through the back door.

She paused in the summer kitchen, which was screened-in during the warm summer months but whose windows were all shuttered now with the approach of winter and listened. Straight ahead lay a dark corridor that ran into the main part of the house's first story.

She could hear old Watt and Carlton Ramsay talking wearily, probably sitting in front of the fire and drinking bourbon that old Watt had shipped in from down south somewhere and that she knew he paid a pretty penny for because of Nash's frequent complaints about it. They were probably drinking and talking over the situation at hand.

Meanwhile, straight beyond the ceiling above her head, she could hear young Zebulon Hollister's sporadic moaning and the creaking of his bedsprings and the complaining of the floorboards beneath the bed.

Two women were speaking in hushed tones up there. Miss Virginia and Mrs. Wolfram. Carrie Anne had seen the Wolfram chaise still parked in front of the lodge when she'd entered the yard from the direction of the old cabin in which she'd left the wounded deputy.

A handsome black man. She'd never been with a black man. She wondered what that would be like. Shame touched her ear tips and it was immediately tempered with a wry humor. She choked back a chuckle, and then, glancing down at her coat pocket to make sure her sewing pouch wasn't visible, she opened the door on her left, stepped through into the well of the staircase that rose to the rear of the second story, and drew the door quietly closed behind her, chewing her lips against the consarned squeaking of the unoiled hinges.

She climbed the stairs that were lit by only the strip of light under the door at the top. She climbed quietly, holding the rail, not wanting to make any noise. As far as she knew, no one had known about her leaving the house either the second or third time when she'd smuggled the wounded deputy out some food and a bottle of

Watt's whiskey. They probably all thought—if they thought about her at all, which she doubted they ever did—that she was where she usually was, in hers and Nash's room, reading or just sitting by the window, darning one of Nash's socks or just staring out the window, dreaming of better days ahead.

She moved through the door, closed it quietly, and glanced at the door to her right. Virginia was reading aloud from her Bible, which she had been doing off and on all day, while Mrs. Wolfram worked on the moaning and groaning Zebulon, for whom the pain in his wounded knee was excruciating. Carrie Anne moved ahead and glanced through the door that was cracked a couple of inches.

Miss Virginia was out of sight but the square-bodied, gray-headed, bespectacled Mrs. Wolfram, a cream shawl draped about her beefy shoulders, was placing a cloth on Zeb's forehead, the young man grabbing at it as if to throw it away.

He was out of his head with fever and misery.

Carrie Anne stepped quietly past the door, entered her own room, and clicked the door closed almost silently behind her. She'd just gotten a lamp lit against the dusky shadows when she heard furtive footsteps in the hall. Her porcelain doorknob turned, the latch clicked, the door opened, and Samuel slipped into the room, wincing as he closed the door even more quietly than she had.

"Sam!' she hissed. "What are you do--?"

But then she was in his arms, and he'd closed his mouth over hers, kissing her. She felt engulfed by the young man—by his arms and broad chest as well as by his big, tender spirit. He was gentler and kinder than Nash. He was like the old Nash whom Carrie Anne had first fallen in love with what seemed a hundred years ago now. Samuel's lips were warm and pliant against hers. Despite the joy she took in his attentions, she wriggled out of his arms.

Keeping her voice low, she said, "Sam, Virginia is in Zeb's room. Not only Virginia but Mrs. Wolfram, too!"

"I know, I know. I'm getting' so tired of hearin' his moanin' and groanin' I feel like puttin' a bullet through his wildcat head."

"Sam!"

Samuel laughed, drew her to him again, kissed her again. As he did, he opened her coat and slid his hands across her belly and bosom. "Oh, Samuel, stop it, please," she urged without heat, continuing to kiss him while trying to pull away.

"Let's do it."

"No."

"Come on."

"Sam, for cryin' out loud—your mother . . .. Oh, Sam . . . how come I can't deny you anything?"

"Because you're gone for me, Carrie Anne. Just like I'm gone for you."

"They'll hear us."

"We'll be quiet."

"No."

"Come on, Carrie Anne. I need you so much; I'm about burstin' at the seams."

He had her dress open now and he'd pushed her camisole up around her neck.

"Oh, Sam. God. If he ever found us. If anyone ever found us . . ."

"Wouldn't be so bad," Samuel said, nuzzling her neck while continuing his fondling. "We'd leave."

"He'd kill us. You know he would. He hardly ever even looks at me, only takes me about once a week, but he won't even look at me, doin' that."

"Shhh. Stop talkin' about him."

"Oh, hell, Sam, we can't . . ."

But then she drew her dress up around her waist and, sitting on the edge of the bed, she quickly shed her drawers. At the same time, Samuel unbuckled his belt and slid his patched denim trousers down to his boots. She let out a lusty chuckle and then lay back on the bed, spreading her legs as he lowered himself between her knees.

They finished in one final, hot gasp of conjoined passion.

Then, as though they both suddenly realized how dangerous was this thing they'd just done, they quickly pulled and pushed and buckled their clothes back into place. While Carrie Anne was standing at the washstand, Samuel came up behind her, wrapped his arms around her, and chewed her left ear.

"Let's pull foot now. Tonight."

"What're you talkin' about?"

"All hell's gonna break loose, Carrie. This ranch is a damn powder keg and the fuse is lit, sizzling and sparkin' only about two inches away from the powder. You hear me? It's over. All Pa and us worked so hard for over the years—it's all dyin' with that deputy we killed." He nuzzled the other side of her neck. "Let's take it as a sign for us to run away together! Get away from old Watt and Nash and that Bible-spoutin' old woman! Hell, not a single one o' them is even gonna care!"

She finished washing and turned around to stare at his chest with a pensive cast to her gaze. "Samuel?"

"What is it?"

"He's not dead."

"Who's not dead?"

"The deputy. He's not dead."

His hands on her shoulders, Samuel searched her eyes. "What're you talkin' about, Carrie Anne?"

"He's out in the old cabin."

<hr />

Stillman stopped Sweets at the base of a low, pine-studded ridge, and hipped around in his saddle, staring back in the direction from which he'd come. Muffled hoof thuds rose softly in the night's dense stillness, stars shimmering in the vast arc of velvet sky from which every scrap of sunlight had long since faded.

Hollister's men were no longer galloping their horses. Stillman had led them into rugged terrain on the backside of the Two-Bears, nearly straight south of the Triple H Connected headquarters. There were many canyons out here, each threaded by a creek that snaked farther south to feed into the Missouri River. There was no way to push a horse very fast through this country without killing it.

Stillman had slowed Sweets as well. Now, he had to take his time, think carefully through his options. He was outnumbered nearly a dozen to one. One misstep, and he would not live to raise his child.

He turned to stare ahead of him. The trail he'd been following along the side of a creek diverged, the left tine snaking off through mixed conifers and deciduous trees, the right tine angling down into the creek. He could see its pale ribbon climbing out of the creek and into the pines. The trail was rocky. He doubted he'd left any noticeable sign—at least none noticeable in the darkness.

When his shadowers reached the fork, they'd likely separate to investigate each tine.

He clucked to Sweets, turning the horse onto the right tine of the fork and dropped down into the creek bed. Only a thin trickle of water murmured and flashed as it angled down the middle of the bed. The bay's hooves clacked sharply on the rocks. On the bed's far side, Sweets sucked a sharp breath as its rider booted him up the steep bank. Soon, the ramrod straight trunks of lodgepole pines closed around them, the thick canopy shutting out the stars.

Stillman had been on this trail before—another old Indian hunting trail, he figured, and one now used by the Triple H Connected riders as it was most likely on Hollister's range. As he climbed the side of the ridge at a slant, he looked up the dark, steeper incline on his right. It took him a while to spy what he was looking for, and when he saw the escarpment rising out of the slope's shoulder, like a small stone castle, he turned Sweets sharply and rode straight up the side of the ridge.

As he approached the escarpment, he could hear the thudding and blowing of the Hollister horses below him. They were probably approaching the forking trails by now. Stillman steered Sweets around to the backside of the dinosaur-like spine of jutting rock, shucked his Henry repeater from its scabbard, and stepped out of the saddle and into a niche amongst the rocks

"Stay, boy," he said softly and began climbing.

He reached the crest of the spiny ridge where a few piñons and cedars twisted from narrow cracks. He made his way across the gently curving top of the ridge to the front where he had a good view of the valley, and dropped to a knee beside a gnarled cedar. He could see the trail, a dark-tan ribbon, meandering through the pines about forty yards back down the slope.

He could hear the hushed voices of the Hollister men conferring farther on down the slope and probably on the other side of the creek. He had a few minutes, so he sat down on his butt, leaning back against a shallow wall of rock, and dug his makings sack from his shirt pocket. His nerves were jangled, and his worry over his deputy wasn't helping.

Rage, more like, he thought.

There was a constant, even, burning throb in both temples, a nagging ache in the pit of his belly. He hadn't fully realized it, but when he'd come upon the three dead men above McMannigle's camp, he'd decided that Leon was likely dead as well. He'd left there wounded and he'd likely died out here . . . somewhere.

Hollister would pay for that. He'd pay dearly.

Stillman paused in the building of his quirley to remove the badge from his shirt and slip it into his coat pocket. For nearly half of his life, he'd considered himself first and foremost a lawman. But out here where outlaws badly outnumbered lawmen, friendship trumped all that.

Leon had saved Stillman's life, and he'd likely died for it. Now, the men who'd killed him would reap their rewards without any tempering by the law. Not that they'd give themselves up if Stillman ordered them to—Nash Hollister had already indicated as much—but Stillman didn't not want to feel bound by any professional authority whatever.

The Hollister riders were going to die tonight, and that's all there was to it.

It was a personal war they'd waged when they'd gone after McMannigle.

The sheriff fired a match to life on his cartridge belt and lit the quirley. He was sitting there smoking, his temper flaring just behind his eyes, when the thudding of a half-dozen horses grew louder. He took another drag from the cigarette, blew it straight out over the valley knowing that there was a good chance his hunters might smell it, and then he mashed the quirley out with the heel of his hand.

He grabbed his Henry and lay prone atop the scarp, staring out over the valley. He doffed his hat, ran a hand through his sweat-damp hair, and quietly levered a live round into the action.

"Come on, fellas," Stillman muttered. "You called the dance, now step to it . . ."

Below him, a horse whinnied. Shod hooves clacked and clattered. As he knew they would, the group split up. Judging by the noise on the trail angling up toward him, he judged at least six of the near dozen men had taken the same fork that he had.

"Whoa," he heard a man say.

"What it is, boss?" asked another.

Hooves thumped. Horses snorted. Stillman saw shadows shifting around on the trail.

"You—J.T. Take the lead."

"Why should I take the lead?"

Stillman could tell that Nash Hollister was trying to keep his voice down but he wasn't doing a very good job. He also thought he detected a thickness in the man's voice, as though he'd been drinking. Stillman didn't doubt that all the men had imbibed in some liquid courage this evening. Tracking a man in the dark was a dangerous bit of work.

"Because I'm *ordering* you to," Nash said. "And I'm *payin'* you to take *orders*. You don't wanna *take* my orders, you don't wanna *take* my money, then you can ride the hell on outta here!"

"Jesus *Christ,*" said a voice that Stillman assumed belonged to J.T. "I was just askin'. Christ!"

Stillman gave a wry snort as the line of shadows began jostling along the trail, heading on up the slope. They were coming up at a slant, angling from his left to his right. He waited until the lead rider, J.T., was at his closest point to the escarpment on which Stillman lay, and then he clicked back his Henry's hammer to full cock. He pressed his cheek up to the rear stock, sited down the barrel.

One of the riders back in the small pack a ways said, "Hey—I smell . . . I smell cigarette smoke!"

"I do, too!" another rider said while one of the silhouetted men jerked so quickly back on his horse's reins that the beast pitched up off its front hooves, losing an angry whinny.

Stillman aimed at one of the silhouettes jostling near the front of the pack, hoping it was Hollister. In the heavy, cool stillness of the autumn night, the Henry roared like the gates of hell being blown off their hinges. A half-second later, Sweets added his own terrified whinny to the echo of Stillman's repeater.

With a feeling like cold water pooling in his belly, Stillman realized his mistake.

The second group of riders hadn't taken the left trail. Knowing the country and anticipating his move, they'd flanked him. Behind him, a spur chinged softly and a stone rolled down the scarp to drop over the ledge before him.

Chapter Nineteen

STILLMAN ROLLED ONTO his back, rose to a half-sitting position, and, seeing the hatted silhouettes of riflemen jostling behind him, opened up with the Henry, the rifle leaping and roaring, flames stabbing from its octagonal barrel.

Men screamed and cursed and performed bizarre death dances, dropping rifles and losing their hats.

When he'd triggered six quick rounds, the brass cartridge casings clattering onto the stone surface of the escarpment, he rolled twice to his right, breathing hard.

He turned onto his belly and opened up on the riders still trying to control their mounts on the trail thirty, forty yards away. When five more empty casings were rolling around the escarpment over his right shoulder, he heaved himself to his feet. As rifles thundered and men shouted on the downslope, he moved at a crouch into a stone breezeway of sorts. It was a shallow trough in the dyke rich with the smell of several cedars twisting amongst deep fissures.

Rifles hammering from the slope clipped one of the cedar's branches and sent it flying, bark pelting Stillman's Stetson.

He moved out of the far side of the shallow corridor and dropped to a knee. Two rifles were flashing in the darkness of the slope, their slugs spanging off the face of the stone corridor.

He aimed just above one of the lapping flashes and squeezed the Henry's trigger. As the rifle bucked against his shoulder, he heard a low grunt and saw a shadow jerk back from the last place he'd seen the rifle flash.

Flames from another rifle lapped toward Stillman. The slug screeched past his left ear. Stillman ran to his right and down the incline of the dyke. A rifle opened up behind him, and Stillman dropped behind a large, square boulder. Two slugs hammered the boulder.

Stillman snaked his Henry around the rock's far side, saw a man-shaped shadow running toward him, starlight winking off the rifle he was extending in his hands. The man stopped, pumped a fresh round into his rifle's chamber with a harsh metallic rasp.

Stillman planted a bead on the center of the shadow.

Boom!

The man cursed and fired his rifle at the scarp's stone surface. The bullet ricocheted off the stony ground between his boots and made a sick, crunching sound as it hammered into the shooter's forehead and blew his hat off. He dropped his rifle and sat down hard, throwing his arms up and out.

Seeing two more shadows moving toward him over the caprock, Stillman pumped a fresh round into his Henry's chamber. Both shadows stopped.

"Crap!" one raked out.

Both men swung around and retreated in the same direction from which they'd come, boots thudding, spurs ringing raucously. Stillman held fire and waited. A few minutes later, hoof thuds rose somewhere ahead on his right, brush crunching under the hooves of the fleeing mounts.

Hollister shouted from downslope, "Where the hell *you boys* goin'?"

More retreating hoof thuds.

"We're done!" one of the riders shouted.

Stillman grinned.

A minute later, the rataplan of more retreating horses rose from the downslope. "Where the hell do you suppose you boys are goin'?" Hollister shouted with even more exasperation, his voice cracking at the end of the question.

"We ain't gettin' paid to get killed by some old mossyhorn lawman with a chip on his shoulder!" A pause filled with fading hoof thuds. "Sorry, boss. Hey, we'll see ya in hell, all right?"

One of the fleeing men hooted loudly, and then they were gone.

Nash Hollister cursed loudly until his voice gave out.

Stillman filled the Henry's loading tube with fresh brash from his cartridge belt, shoved the tube back into place beneath the barrel, locked it, cocked the sixteen-shot repeater, and moved out from behind his boulder. "Sounds like it's just us, Hollister. Let's finish it!"

The reply from the downslope was one more set of horse hooves dwindling into the distance.

⁓⌣⌐

Samuel Hollister placed his hands around Carrie Anne's upper arms. "What did you say?"

"The deputy's alive." She glanced at the door to make sure no one was listening, and then dropped her voice another octave. "He's out in the cabin."

"H-how, Carrie Anne? How . . . ?"

"He rode into the yard earlier. Er . . . I mean, his horse carried him here. He was riding that big roan Blaze always rode." Blaze. She had to admit she'd sort of liked the way Westin looked at her sometimes, but of course she hadn't let on. Doing so might have gotten her horse-whipped.

But Blaze was probably dead now. No loss to the world, because most of the time he had flat, evil eyes, and he mistreated his horses and he was always throwing horse apples at Barney when none of the Hollister men were around, but still, Carrie Anne had to admit that she'd liked the glinting admiration in his eyes when he saw her walking out to the well or to the stable. He'd been smart enough to never speak to her, however.

"Holy hell!"

Carrie Anne rose onto her toes and pressed two fingers to her lips. *"Shhh!"*

Samuel winced and glanced at the door. "He's alive?"

"Of course, he's alive. I'm not housing a dead man out there. What would be the point?"

"How bad is he hurt?"

"Not real bad. Took a bullet in his leg. He got the bullet out himself, but it grieves him something awful. I sewed up the wound, brought him a bottle of Watt's whiskey." Carrie Anne forced her mouth into a straight line, suppressing a smile.

Samuel turned to the door. "I'm goin' out there."

Carrie Anne ran to him. "What for?"

Samuel stopped with one hand on the doorknob. "I gotta get him out of there. What if Nash finds him? He'll kill him. If I can get him to town, I might be able to save the ranch. Not that I really give a damn about it, anymore. But I don't wanna be a part of killin' an innocent man, and I would be, because I was there when Nash ambushed him. Besides, I'd hate to see all we worked for get plowed under by the evil ways of Nash and that demented old man!"

Samuel stared at Carrie Anne, thoughtful. "Pack a bag. I'll pack one, too. Then we'll hitch a wagon, drive down to the cabin, pick up the deputy, and take him to town. Then we'll buy train tickets—I got some money saved up--and get the hell away from here. Just you and me, Carrie Anne!"

"Oh, my god! Samuel, I don't know!"

"What choice do we have? When Watt doesn't find that lawman out in the mountains, he might think to look in the cabin. Probably not tonight, but I won't be able to sleep, anyway, worryin' about it."

Samuel took the girl in his arms again and kissed her. "Do you love me Carrie Anne?"

Her eyes grew wide, serious. "Do you love me?"

"I think I do, sure. Yes, I think I do."

Carrie Anne swallowed, nodded. Her heart was racing. It seemed like she'd finally found a way to change her miserable life. "All right," she said. "I'll pack my bag. You pack yours, and we'll meet in the summer kitchen."

Samuel kissed her and slipped out the door and into the hall.

Chapter Twenty

MCMANNIGLE WAS TORN from a deep and dreamless sleep by the squawk of door hinges and a chilly draft wafting over him. He snapped his head up, grabbing the pistol he'd placed beside his right leg on the cot.

"Don't shoot, Deputy!" Carrie Anne said, flinching.

Leon blinked. For a second, he thought he was seeing double, but then he saw that she wasn't alone. She'd come with one of the Hollister sons—the middle one, Samuel, who was dressed in a long, quilted deerskin coat and cream Stetson. His curly brown hair fell down to nearly his shoulders. His wide, blue eyes shone in the light of the candle lantern that the girl had left lit on the table beside the cot.

Leaving the door open, the young man placed his hands on the girl's shoulders, and gently

pushed her aside. "It's all right," he said to Mc-
Mannigle, holding his gloved hands up in suppli-
cation. "I'm here to help."

"Help?" Leon groused, skeptically.

"No one else is here. Just me and Carrie Anne.
We aim to get you to town, to that sawbones,
Evans. I don't want any more trouble, Mister."
Samuel glanced over his right shoulder, toward
where a horse and buckboard wagon stood out in
the breezy darkness beyond the cabin's dilapidated stoop. "We got a wagon, plenty of blankets in it
to keep you warm on the way to town."

Leon glanced from the boy to Carrie Anne
and back again. He canted his head to one side.
"Why?"

"Cause it's the right thing to do," said Carrie
Anne, striding forward.

As she approached Leon to place a hand across
his forehead, he depressed his Smith & Wesson's
hammer and slid the revolver into the holster
hanging off the back of the chair beside him.
"Still got a fever, I'm afraid. Not as bad as before,
though. How do you feel? Do you think you can
make it to town?"

"Hell, yes! Uh . . . pardon my French, Miss Carrie Anne." Leon chuckled as he slung the blankets
back and dropped his stockinged feet to the floor.

"That's all right," Carrie Anne said. "We don't

hold to much with form out here at the Triple H Connected."

"That's for sure," said Samuel, moving toward Leon. "Let me help you."

Leon's blood froze in his veins when he saw a shadow move in the open doorway. A floorboard creaked beneath a heavy tread, and a deep voice said, "Well, now, ain't this cozy?"

Carrie Anne gasped and swung toward Nash Hollister standing in the doorway, a cocked revolver aimed toward her, Leon, and Samuel. Samuel swung around to face his brother. Leon reached for his holstered Smithy but froze when he realized he didn't have a chance.

Nash curled one side of his upper lip, as though daring him to pull the hogleg from the holster. Leon lowered his arm, rested his hand on his left thigh.

Damn.

Nash took two slope steps into the cabin, keeping his lip curled and flaring his nostrils as he studied his brother and his wife. "Seen you leave the barn in the wagon. I was just ridin' in." He took one more step, sliding his cocked Colt between Carrie Anne and Samuel. "What in the hell do you two corkheaded tinhorns think you're doin'?"

"Nash, please," Carrie Anne said.

"I asked you a question, *wife!*"

Carrie Anne stomped one foot and clenched her fists at her sides. "I ain't no wife to you! Any more than you been a husband to me after we found out I was barren!" She clamped a hand over her mouth as though in shock over what had spewed from it.

Nash stared at her for a time. He slid his shocked gaze to Samuel and then back to Carrie Anne.

"So, you took up with my little brother. My chicken-hearted little brother. Ain't this prime? Ain't this prime? And you were both gonna save the Negro here and send your family to hell!" Nash laughed maniacally, aiming his pistol at his wife straight out from his shoulder. He seemed totally surprised, as though even with them all living under the same roof together, he hadn't had an inkling about what had been going on between his younger brother and his wife. "You lyin', cheatin' little *doxie!*"

Samuel threw up his arms and stepped between Carrie Anne and his brother. "Stop it, Nash!"

Nash was gritting his teeth. His revolver thundered.

"No!" Carrie Anne screamed.

Samuel yelped and flew back against the girl.

At the same time, Leon bounded off the cot, ignoring the ripping pain in his right thigh, and lunged for his pistol hanging off the chair back. He was sluggish from sleep and from the shock of the situation, so he wasn't moving as lithely as he'd wanted to.

Carrie Anne was screaming. Samuel was bellowing. Nash's pistol roared again, and the slug curled the air beside Leon's left ear and smashed into the wall behind him. He pulled his revolver from his holster, tripped over his own feet, and fell to the floor.

The fall probably prevented him from taking Hollister's next shot to the forehead. Instead, the slug hammered the chair, knocking it over. Sitting on the floor on his butt, Leon extended the Smith & Wesson toward Nash who was glaring through the wafting powder smoke, trying to draw another bead on the deputy.

Leon's Smithy flashed and roared.

Nash yelped and stumbled backward, clutching his left shoulder. He spun around, dropped to a knee, and then, bellowing like a poleaxed bull, heaved himself to both feet and stumbled out the door and into the night.

"Sam!" Carrie Anne was screaming, crouched over the young man flopping around on the cabin floor. *"Samuel!"*

"Let me have a look at him." Leon dropped to his good knee beside Carrie Anne and pulled her up off the boy she'd been sprawled across, sandwiching his face in her hands. Blood spotted the young man's left shoulder. "Shove some cloth into that bullet wound. He'll be all right!"

Pushing himself to his feet with a wince, clutching his revolver in his right hand, he began dragging his right foot toward the open door.

Hearing the girl rip the hem of her camisole, the deputy headed on out the door and then pressed his back against the cabin's front wall in case Hollister was waiting for him out here. When no shot came, he pushed away from the wall and stumbled out into the yard behind the wagon and the whickering horse in the traces.

Groans and the sounds of crunching brush rose to his left and he turned to see a silhouetted figure stumbling along the trail that led toward the main Hollister house.

McMannigle raised his revolver. "Hollister!"

The shambling, grunting figure continue to jostle away from him.

Leon fired. He fired again, once more, and watched the uncertain figure stumble over the top of a rise and out of sight. At the same time, the horse whinnied sharply to the deputy's right, and galloped away, pulling the clattering wagon along behind it.

Leon cursed and started limping after Hollister, gritting his teeth and grunting with each painful, dragging step.

As he moved down the trail, he could occasionally see Nash Hollister's shamble-footed prints in the dirt, and the frequent glint of blood on fallen yellow leaves. He continued dragging his bad right leg along the trail, down through a shallow valley and then up and over the next hill and into the ranch yard. As he passed between the blacksmith shop and the corral in which several horses milled in the darkness, whickering curiously, he turned toward the main house.

Hollister had just gained the steps and he was pulling himself up onto the porch by the rail, stumbling as though drunk. He lifted his head, and his agonized voice echoed around the otherwise silent ranch yard, "Open . . . open the damn door!" There was a loud bang, as though he kicked the door with his boot.

McMannigle continued toward the house, raising his pistol and clicking back the hammer. Hoof thuds rose to his right. A familiar voice yelled, "Hold it!"

Leon turned to see a large man sitting what appeared a bay horse just inside the ranch portal, aiming a pistol at him. The deputy recognized the high-crowned, tan Stetson and buckskin mackinaw of Ben Stillman.

"Ben!" Leon cried, lowering his own revolver. "Christ almighty!"

Stillman kicked Sweets into an instant gallop toward Leon, who threw up his left arm toward the house. "Hollister!"

⌒‿⌒

Stillman swung his bay toward the house as the door opened, showing dull umber light and a tall, jostling figure silhouetted again it. The door closed and then there was the hollow pop of a gun being triggered inside the lodge. A woman screamed shrilly. There was a heavy thud as though that of a body hitting the floor.

Stillman leaped down from his saddle in front of the house, dropped his reins, and took the veranda steps two at a time. He pulled the door open and stood just inside the doorway, crouching and aiming his cocked Colt into the broad, warm space before him filled with the tang of pine smoke from the crackling hearth and the range.

Nash Hollister lay twisted on one side about six feet away. His eyes were half-open, his hat was off, and blood was tricking down both sides of his head, matting his hair. There was a puddle of it on the front of his coat. Old Watt Hollister stood to the right, inside the parlor area of the large, open first story of the lodge. He held a smoking Remington revolver in his right hand, which he was slowly lowering as he stared in wide-eyed shock and befuddlement at his dead eldest son.

Hollister's housekeeper, the old cowboy Carlton Ramsay, was down on one knee beside Nash. He, too, stared in shock at the deceased son. Meanwhile, Virginia stood atop the steps that ran up the right side of the kitchen, clamping her hands to her face, screaming. "No! Not Nash, too! Oh, noooo—not Nash, too!"

Stillman lowered his pistol and walked over and snatched Watt's smoking Schofield from the old man's arthritic hand. Hollister appeared numb. He sagged back into a rocking chair behind him, glancing at Stillman and muttering, "I . . . thought . . . he . . . was . . . you . . ."

Then he returned his stricken gaze to his dead son once more and said nothing more.

Chapter Twenty-One

TOMMY DILLOUGHBOY LIFTED his head from his pillow in Doc Evans's spare bedroom and blinked his eyes. Bright sunlight shone in the dormer window over his right shoulder. Loud, happily chirping birds darted past the window, flicking shadows through the golden sunshine splashing onto the throw rug on the floor beside the bed.

"Holy hell," Tommy said, squinting as he glanced out the window. "What the hell time is it?"

He looked around but he saw no clock. He didn't own a watch. He'd wanted to get a jump on the day. A jump on the doc, that was. But, judging by the muffled snores resonating faintly through the floor, Doc Evans was still sawing logs.

No wonder. The man had sat up drinking until late last night. Tommy had heard him down

there from time to time, clinking a bottle against
a glass as he'd refreshed his brandy. The doctor
had staggered up the stairs once to check on
Tommy and to replace the poultice on the young
man's bullet wound, which he also smeared with
arnica. Tommy had been amazed at how handy
the sawbones was, even three sheets to the wind.

The pill roller had done a good job on him.
Tommy felt relatively strong, and the wound in
his side only pained him a little. Not bad. He
could probably ride.

Once he acquired a horse . . .

Tommy sat up and dropped his feet to the floor.
He rose slowly, not wanting to rip the stitches
open. He had to get out of here fast, before Stillman learned he was here. If Stillman got wind of
his presence in Clantick, the sheriff would likely
put two and two together and figure out that
Tommy had been the one rustler who'd gotten
away from Stillman and his deputy Friday night.

Gotten away with a bullet in his side, that was.

Tommy had to light a shuck out of Clantick or
he'd likely be spending the next fifteen years in
the state pen down in Deer Lodge. Slowly, carefully, he dressed, wrapped his gun and cartridge
belt around his waist, and carried his boots
downstairs. He found a pair of saddlebags hanging over a chair back in the doctor's kitchen, and,

listening to the doctor snoring in his bedroom off the parlor, he quietly scrounged the kitchen for trail supplies.

When he'd stuffed as many airtight tins of canned fruits and vegetables, coffee, flour, sugar, and biscuits as the saddlebags would hold, he donned his boots near the front door, and went out.

The morning was cool, and an inch of feathery snow had fallen overnight, but the sun was high, and it would likely warm up to above freezing. It would be a good day for riding. He'd ride south, maybe hole up in Denver for the winter. Come spring, he'd continue on down to Mexico.

But first he needed a horse. And then he needed a stake.

He tramped out to Evans's stable and saddled Evans' horse—a beefy, hammer-headed chestnut. The horse obviously had too much weight on him for a long ride, but Tommy would trade the mount for a better one farther on down the trail. The horse whickered several times as Tommy saddled him, obviously not too pleased about the stranger strapping the doctor's saddle on his back. The lazy beast had probably planned on spending the day right here in his little stable and connecting pen, close to his hay and oats.

Tommy worked tensely, hoping Evans would

not awaken and look out his window and find
him stealing his horse. He kept cooing and patting the horse, trying to soothe the obviously
peeved beasts's nerves, hoping the horse didn't let
loose a warning whinny that would awaken the
sawbones. He'd hate to have to shoot the doctor
after all Evans had done for him.

He puffed out his cheeks and blew a deep,
relieved sigh as ten minutes later he rode the
horse to the bottom of the bluff that the doctor's
rambling house sat upon and headed on to the
edge of town. He'd been about to swing south
to avoid the main street, so he wouldn't be seen
by either Stillman or his deputy, but then he saw
a familiar figure tramping toward the Drovers
Saloon. At the same time, he remembered that
the Triple H Connected riders had said Stillman
wasn't in town, and that they'd been searching
for his deputy.

Maybe neither one was back yet. Or maybe the
Triple H Connected riders had caught up with
them both, and they'd never be back . . .

Tommy quirked his right cheek in a specula-
tive, fleeting grin.

Tommy's heart thumped anxiously as he
watched Elmer Burke mount the broad veranda
of the Drover's Saloon and fish in his trouser
pocket for the keys to the saloon's winter door.

Burke wore a wool coat over his portly frame, and a deerskin cap with wool earflaps obscured his face. Tommy's heart increased its frenetic pace as he watched Burke unlock the saloon's door, stomp snow from his boots, and go on inside.

Today was Sunday, if Tommy hadn't lost all track. That meant that Burke had probably taken in a handsome amount of cash last night. That cash was probably tucked away in the safe that Burke had in his office. Tommy knew about the safe from having scouted the Drovers for a possible holdup last spring.

When the saloon owner had gotten his door open, Tommy touched his holstered gun through the skirt of his wool coat and booted the big chestnut forward. He gazed at the sheriff's office and was relieved to see no prints in the snow fronting the place and no smoke curling from either of the two tin chimney pipes sprouting from the shake-shingled roof.

He pulled the horse up to one of the hitchracks, dismounted, and slung the reins over the rack. He looked around, hitching up his pants and trying to look casual. It being Sunday morning, no one else appeared out this early except three mongrel dogs rummaging around between two buildings on the other side of the street, the smallest one nipping commandingly at the other two.

Smoke wafted from a few of the main street business buildings that also served as homes and from houses flanking the main drag. Smoke also lifted from Sam Wa's just down the street. The old Chinaman, being a heathen, probably worked on Sunday. In fact, he and Evelyn were probably getting ready for the after-church crowd. Squeeze the Christians even on their Day of Rest. That was the Chinaman's way.

Tommy Dilloughboy snickered. He lifted the skirt of his coat and pulled his Schofield .44 from its holster. He held the pistol down low against his thigh as he mounted the veranda fronting the Drovers. As he turned the knob of the winter door set behind the batwings and pushed the door open, he raised the pistol and flicked the hammer back.

He stepped inside, squinting into the dingy shadows, and quickly, quietly closed the door behind him. The saloon was lit by only the golden light pushing through the windows. Where the bright light didn't reach was all thick, purple shadows. He looked toward the massive, ornate bar and back bar running down the room's right side but did not see Burke.

Then a voice called from a half-open door at the back of the room. "Can't you read the sign? I'm closed. This is Sunday. Won't be open till noon!"

Tommy recognized the room from which Burke's irritated voice had emanated. It was Burke's office. He'd probably come in to get a jump on his books.

"I know that, Mr. Burke," Tommy called, walking slowly down the room along the bar, holding his cocked revolver straight out in front of him. "This is an emergency."

"Emergency?" Behind the half-open door, a swivel chair chirped and boots thumped. "What the hell you talkin' about—an emergen-" The burly saloon owner cut himself off when he peered through the door and saw Tommy walking toward him. Burke scowled, nose reddening.

"What in the hell are you doin' here, Dilloughboy? Put that damn gun down!"

"I don't think so." Tommy quickened his pace. "Step back away from the door, Burke. You try to close it on me, I'll blast it open. Get them hands raised!"

Burke raised his hands and stepped back away from the door. Tommy moved inside the room, rife with the smell of cigar smoke, and closed the door behind him. Burke stood facing him. His broad, pale face framed by bushy, sandy-colored muttonchops was crimson with fury, wide eyes hesitant, apprehensive. Tommy looked the portly man over. When he was sure that Burke wasn't carrying a weapon, he looked at the safe sitting against the far wall beyond Burke's roll-top desk cluttered with papers and an open ledger. A cigar rested in a wooden ashtray, unfurling a skein of smoke toward the room's grime-stained ceiling.

Tommy studied the safe and grinned. He'd thought he'd have to force Burke to open it, which would take time, but the door was open about seven inches.

Burke was reading Tommy's devious mind. "Forget it, kid."

"You forget it." Tommy waved the gun at Burke. "Step back or I'll blast ya." He gave a menacing wink. "You don't think I will, just try me. I'm flat broke and out of options."

Burke's broad nostrils flared. He glanced at the pistol aimed at his bulging belly behind a blue wool shirt, its tails untucked. He swallowed and, keeping his pudgy hands raised, sidestepped toward his desk. Keeping his gun aimed at the saloon owner, Tommy backed to the safe, dropped to one knee, and shoved the door wide.

Bright sunlight from the two windows flanking the safe spilled into the safe's dark interior, revealing several good-sized stacks of unbanded greenbacks. There had to be several thousand dollars in there.

"I work for a livin', kid," Burke said. "Why don't you try it?"

"Shut up," Tommy said mildly, taking quick, darting looks inside the safe as he scooped the money out with his free left hand, keeping his Schofield aimed at Burke with his other hand.

"You devil," Burke said through a snarl as, panting with excitement, eyes bright with greedy merriment, Tommy stuffed the money into his coat pockets.

"Yeah," Tommy laughed. "Yeah, you could say that. You wouldn't be wrong."

Having emptied the safe into his pockets, the leathery, inky smell of the bills filling his nose and making his mouth water, a pouch of coins weighing down his right coat pocket, Tommy straightened and walked over to where Burke scowled at him by his desk.

"Yeah, you could say that," Tommy said, raising his pistol high above his head. Bringing the butt of the revolver down at an arc, he grunted savagely, "But it wouldn't be one bit polite!"

The butt of the Schofield smacked down hard against Burke's left temple. The saloon owner grunted and fell back against his desk, flailing with his hands to stay upright, blinking his eyes. But then he lost consciousness, sagged sideways, and hit the floor with a heavy thud and a rattling sigh.

Tommy gave a whoop, swung around, opened

the door, and ran into the saloon's main drinking hall.

"Hold it, Tommy!"

He stopped dead in his tracks.

"Evelyn!"

She stood a third of the way down the bar from the saloon's open front door. She was somewhat silhouetted against the bright windows and the door behind her, but he could see that it was Evelyn, sure enough. She wore a long, ratty wool coat, and her braided, blond hair hung down past her shoulders. Her light-blue eyes shone in the sunlight angling across her face.

She was holding a double-barreled shotgun that must have weighed nearly as much as she did, straight out from her right shoulder. Her head was canted toward the breech, and she was aiming down the barrel.

"Drop your pistol, Tommy," she ordered firmly, clicking both rabbit ear hammers back to full cock and scowling down the heavy weapon that she held with surprising steadiness.

~～⁔～

Evelyn felt a knife twist in her guts, but she kept her hands wrapped tightly around the shotgun, her right index finger curled through the trigger guard.

"Nah, nah, nah, nah," Tommy said, that grin of his dimpling his cheeks as he started walking slowly along the bar. "You put that big ole barn blaster down. You don't wanna shoot me, Evelyn. It's Tommy, fer chrissakes!"

He chuckled and held his hands out from his sides, keeping his revolver in the right one.

"You're a miserable human being, Tommy. You're a horse-thief and a common robber. If you don't stop right there, I'm going to put you out of everyone's misery."

"Ah, come, Evelyn. I got over a thousand dollars in my pockets. Maybe several thousand. Just think how far we could get with all that money!"

"Stop walking, Tommy."

"Evelyn, be reasonable."

"Stop walking, Tommy."

He must have read the seriousness in her eyes. The gravity in her tone. He stopped about ten feet away from her. He continued to hold his arms half out from his sides, about chest high, the pistol in the right one. It was like he was just showing her the gun, not outright threatening her with it.

But the threat was there. Even in his smiling, deep-brown eyes, in his dimpled cheeks, the threat was there.

"Toss it away," Evelyn ordered softly, grimly. "I'm takin' you to the jailhouse, Tommy. I'm turnin' the key on you. See, I'm the temporary deputy sheriff. I was headin' over to the jailhouse to stoke the cellblock stove when I saw the doc's horse, Faustus, standing outside."

"You're a deputy sheriff?"

Evelyn smiled without mirth as she continued aiming down the shotgun's twin barrels. "Ain't that a laugh? Drop it, Tommy, or I'll blast you to hell."

He studied her. The smile left his lips as well as his eyes. He narrowed his lids and turned his head slightly to one side. "Evelyn, think about it. Think about what a good time we could have—you an' me."

"You're scum, Tommy."

"Evelyn..."

"You got one more second."

His face became a mask of cold evil. He swung the revolver toward Evelyn, but before he could click the hammer back, Elmer Burke, who'd crept up behind him, smashed a hide-wrapped bungstarter down hard against the back of the young firebrand's head.

Tommy was out before he hit the floor at Evelyn's feet. Burke sagged against the bar, holding a blood-spotted handkerchief against his head.

Evelyn sighed as she lowered the shotgun, depressing the heavy hammers.

"You all right, Elmer?"

"Yeah, yeah. Thanks, Evelyn."

"I'll fetch the doc. You're gonna need a stitch or two there."

Elmer just leaned back against the bar, holding the handkerchief against his forehead and staring angrily down at the unconscious Tommy Dilloughboy.

Evelyn didn't give the young outlaw so much as another look. She set Sam Wa's shotgun atop the bar and headed outside.

She stopped on the stoop to see that a wagon had pulled up in front of the Drovers. Stillman's horse, Sweets, was tied to the wagon's tailgate. Three people were riding in the back, on a mound of skins and furs. Leon was one of them, staring toward Evelyn with a question in his eyes. The other two were a pretty young, brown-haired woman and a Hollister boy. The middle one, with curly brown hair. The Hollister boy sat back against the wagon's front panel, a blanket pulled up to his neck. He was staring at her skeptically. The girl, whom Evelyn had never seen before, sat close beside him holding a comforting hand on his chest.

Ben Stillman had dismounted the wagon and was walking toward Evelyn from the wagon's far side and around Sweets, boots crunching in the light dusting of snow.

"Evelyn?"

"Oh, Ben!" she said, tears washing over her eyes. Tears of sorrow, tears of guilt, tears of relief at seeing that Ben and Leon were all right.

"I was headin' for the doc's place when I saw Faustus standin' out here. What in the . . . ?" Stillman paused, studying her incredulously from the bottom of the steps. "What happened, girl?"

"Oh, nothin' really." Evelyn ran down the steps, wrapped her arms around Stillman's waist, and pressed her cheek against his buckskin coat, squeezing him.

She convulsed with a sob.

She laughed through her tears. "I just took down an outlaw for you, that's all!"

A Look at: Into The Breech
(Ben Stillman Book 10)

FROM THE CURRENT KING OF THE WILD
AND WOOLY, BEST-SELLING
WESTERN SERIES!

When Doctor Clyde Evans is kidnapped from his home in the middle of the night to tend to a wounded outlaw, Sheriff Ben Stillman's problems are only just beginning. Stillman tracks the doctor to a remote cabin deep in the Two-Bear Mountains. He springs the doctor, shoots the outlaws, and confiscates the bank loot. He also arrests a beautiful young outlaw, Hettie Styles, who promptly puts a bounty on Stillman's head.

Compounding the sheriff's problems, his old foe Jacob Henry Battles rides into town with a steel hook replacing the arm Stillman shot off years ago, before sending Battles to prison. Dying from consumption, the vengeance-seeking old outlaw challenges Stillman to a deadly game of cat and mouse.

For fans of William W. Johnstone and George P. Cosmatos's Tombstone, you'll love the tenth novel in the epic, fast-paced Sheriff Ben Stillman series.

**AVAILABLE NOW ON AMAZON
FROM PETER BRANDVOLD AND WOLFPACK
PUBLISHING**

About the Author

PETER BRANDVOLD grew up in the great state of North Dakota in the 1960's and '70s, when television westerns were as popular as shows about hoarders and shark tanks are now, and western paperbacks were as popular as *Game of Thrones.*

Brandvold watched every western series on television at the time. He grew up riding horses and herding cows on the farms of his grandfather and many friends who owned livestock.

Brandvold's imagination has always lived and will always live in the West. He is the author of over a hundred lightning-fast action westerns under his own name and his pen name, Frank Leslie.

Lightning Source UK Ltd.
Milton Keynes UK
UKHW011325051120
372850UK00004B/1363